JUSTIN TIME

Justin Time

Shane A. Aldrich

iUniverse, Inc.

New York Lincoln Shanghai

Justin Time

iUniverse books may be ordered through booksellers or by contacting:

iUniverse
2021 Pine Lake Road, Suite 100
Lincoln, NE 68512
www.iuniverse.com
1-800-Authors (1-800-288-4677)

Because of the dynamic nature of the Internet, any Web addresses or links contained in this book may have changed since publication and may no longer be valid.

This is a work of fiction. All of the characters, names, incidents, organizations, and dialogue in this novel are either the products of the author's imagination or are used fictitiously.

ISBN: 978-0-595-47810-1

Printed in the United States of America

For Jennifer, who I have the great fortune to have not only as my wife and mother of our children, but also as my best friend.

CHAPTER 1

─────────── ▼ ───────────

Before my mother died at the age of forty-two, she confided in me her deepest, darkest secret. Japhet Thyme, the man I had called Father for twenty-one years, was in fact, not my real father at all. My mother had been pregnant with me when they met, and assuming I was his, they had married soon after they had begun dating. My mother confided all of this and more to me in her final days.

"Justin," she had whispered weakly to me that early spring afternoon, "Justin, there is something I want you to know ... before I ... I want you to know the truth."

Dead at forty-two of cervical cancer. Dead less than a week after she had decided to tell me the truth about facts I had been oblivious to before. I remember that day so well, it had been a cold spring day. Sleet had made an incessant tapping noise at her sterile hospital room window. The cloying scent of fading flowers and fading life had filled the air. I remember feeling helpless and hopeless. The doctors had told those of us in her immediate family that it was only a matter of time.

Time. Ironic how that was also my last name only with a different spelling. Ironic that Japhet Thyme, the man I had thought was my father, in all of his infinite wisdom and twisted sense of humor had decided to name me Justin.

Suffice and needless to say, I was teased without mercy throughout my elementary school career. In high school as an outlet, I had reveled in contact sports. I had played football in the fall, ice hockey in the winter, and lacrosse in the spring. I still kept the newspaper clipping of my overtime goal in the State Championship lacrosse game from my Junior year. It read, *Justin Thyme Scores Just in Time.*

Japhet Thyme had never been much of a father figure for me. While I had been off involved with girls and sports, he had been busy trying to get his fledgling computer business off the ground. We did not grow any closer over the years, as it became apparent to even me that there was not any physical resemblance between the two of us. Nor much similarity between my mother and I, for that matter.

"You look just like your father," she had confided in me during one of our confessional sessions. Her slender hand had risen from the bed like a pale cobra and caressed my cheek. "His name was Erich Craigie, and I wasn't much older than you when we met."

She seemed to doze off, or perhaps she was just remembering. I looked up and found myself staring at my reflection through the open door and into her bathroom mirror. I had straight dark hair and gray eyes. I had what amounted to a year-round tan, and I had often wondered if there were some Native American ancestry in my lineage.

My mind had raced. Erich Craigie? Neither of my parents had ever mentioned that name before, at least around me. Who was he? How had they met? What did he do? What was he like?

Her eyes opened, "Justin?"

"Yes Mother?"

It was so difficult to accept that the vibrant woman of my youth was only days away from death.

"Your real father, his name was Erich Craigie."

"You've already said that, Mother," I replied, gently reminding her. The pain medicine that the doctors had her on did not exactly make her coherent at all times, and her memory was sometimes in question. While the drugs did not make her delusional, coherency was often a problem.

"I loved him. At twenty-one I had found the one true love of my life. You understand what I'm saying, don't you?"

Indeed I did. Her name was Brianna Hawthorne. Bree and I had even discussed the m-word several times. We were due to graduate from Maryland University together in May. Was my mother also implying however, that she had never truly loved Japhet Thyme? My mind was reeling from all of these revelations.

Then my mother did go to sleep. She simply nodded off with all of the suddenness and efficiency of someone living with narcolepsy. I returned the next day, and after placing the cheap bouquet of flowers I had procured from the gift shop on the table next to her bed, I had gently spoken her name to see if she were awake.

"Erich?" There was hope in her voice. Perhaps she had been dreaming.

"No, Mother. It's me, Justin" Then I added to be helpful, "your son."

"Of course you're my son. I'm not that far gone. Yet."

"How did you and Erich meet?"

She arranged her pillows into a more comfortable position. I moved to help and she waved me off. Satisfied, she spoke slowly at first, "I was on my way to the Atlantic Scientific Institute in Bermuda for my internship in marine biology. The ship I was on sank. He rescued me."

"So, he was a member of the Coast Guard or something?"

"He was," she paused and smiled. "He was an aggressive salvager."

"A what? What do you mean by that?"

"Erich Craigie was a pirate."

I frowned in consternation. I thought perhaps I should speak to the doctors about the strength of her medication. My mother had never been prone to flights of fancy or wild imaginings. Her eyes were very clear, and there was conviction in her voice.

"You do realize what you are saying, don't you?"

With a trace of anger in her voice she replied, "Yes, Justin, I'm sure. I was rescued by modern day pirates while sailing through the Bermuda Triangle. I spent almost three months with them, and during that time I fell in love with their captain—your father."

She sighed and seemed to sink deeper into her pillows, as if this had all been too much at once for her. "Mother?" Even I was able to hear the alarm in my voice. I was reaching for the Nurse Call button when she turned and looked up at me. There was so much I wanted, needed to ask her.

"I'm fine, Son. As fine as I can be."

"How did you, how did you get—back?"

Cara Nichole Owens Thyme, the woman I had ever really known as 'Mother,' seemed to gather her strength before speaking. Her voice was surprisingly clear. "Have you ever heard the expression that if you love something, set it free? If it comes back to you, it's yours. If it doesn't come back, it was never love at all?" I nodded. "He let me go. And even though I did love him, I never went back. And now it's too late." There was a hitch in her voice. She swallowed with some difficulty and I handed her a styrofoam cup of water. Her hands shook as she took the cup and sipped tentatively.

"What happened?" was all I could ask.

"Life." She closed her eyes. "Life happened," she repeated. "I came home, spent some time with your grandmother—my mother, and then—got on with life. I was a survivor," she added in a cryptic tone of voice.

"But, if you loved him …?" I let the question hang between us.

Her eyes opened. "I did, and still do. But his love—it frightened me. It was so simple, and pure. With Erich everything was reduced to the lowest common denominator. I know how foolish this must all sound to you."

Thinking of Bree, I answered, "No. No it doesn't sound foolish at all."

"I found a job at the Maryland Aquarium, and met Japhet who was on the board of directors. He was a bit older than I, but we began dating. Several months into the relationship we realized we—I was pregnant. Assuming the child was his, we got married."

I leaned forward in the cushioned hospital chair I was sitting in. Why is it that even the padded chairs in a hospital are uncomfortable?

"Does Dad—Japhet, know any of this?"

She shook her head. "He knows only the story I told the world—that I was shipwrecked and managed to row my way to a shipping lane where I was rescued by a Coast Guard Cutter."

"Does he know that I'm not really his son?"

"I think he suspects, but he would never say anything. You're his only male heir, and he does care a great deal about you. He achieved a lot through you vicariously that he wouldn't have otherwise been able to do. You'll inherit his fortune some day. I guess Erich was right."

"I don't understand."

She smiled. "Japhet was never an athlete. He was overweight and asthmatic. Through you he experienced sports and all the glory that goes with them. Japhet and his chain of computer stores are worth several million dollars. The business, and the money, will all be yours someday."

I was an only child, so that made sense, but running a chain of computer stores? "I have a degree, or will have a degree in Education. I was thinking of being a teacher."

Again she smiled, with pride this time, and nodded. "A noble choice, Justin. But there isn't any money in teaching, even if you went on to become a professor at a college. Teachers aren't respected anymore, they're an easy scapegoat for everything that's wrong with society. It isn't enough to just be a teacher either. You have to be a surrogate parent, doctor, lawyer, referee, coach, psychologist, and on and on."

Trying to make a joke I said, "But I would get summers off."

"No, you wouldn't. My cousin Courtney was a teacher. She spent summers taking recertification courses, teaching Summer School, and planning for the following year. Teachers do not get all the vacation days people think they do. Most people work nine to five and go home. Cort used to begin her day at six thirty, and was often at school until after five because of meetings and planning. Then she would spend her whole weekend grading papers."

"It's more important to me to do something that I would love, rather than make a lot of money."

"I know, Justin. I'm not saying teaching is a bad profession, I just want you to know what you are getting into. Half of all teachers don't even last five years."

"If it didn't work out, couldn't I just take over then? Or even sell the corporation?"

She shook her head. "In Japhet's will it specifies that if you do not want the company, then the board can elect to buy it. You would still get a little over a million dollars after all is said and done, but you would still be better off assuming the leadership role he has set up for you."

"So I don't have a choice?"

"Of course you do. It is your life, after all. But Japhet is going to retire in a couple of years. He's hoping when you graduate in May, you'll intern at one of the stores and gradually take over. Of course, he may remarry once I'm—gone, and if he has another child or children, anything could happen then."

"You also said something about Erich being right?"

She exhaled loudly through her nose, a barely repressed laugh. This lead to a coughing episode and her face turned red. With one, final loud cough, she answered, "He usually was right. He once told me that if I returned to civilization, I could look forward to a nine to five job, a house with a white picket fence, a husband who didn't appreciate me, and tediousness. He also said there isn't anyone who has any real control over his destiny."

I wriggled uncomfortably in my seat. He had been talking about her, but was she now talking about me? Was that all I had to look forward to for the rest of my life? Another question arose unbidden in my mind, if my mother had known at the time that she would be dead in less than two dozen years, would she have remained with Erich? I was about to put voice to these thoughts when she quietly said, "Honey? I'm really tired. Maybe you should get going now?"

I kissed her goodbye and then made my way through the lonely halls of the hospital to the parking garage. I slid behind the wheel of a forest green BMW—an early graduation present from my father—from Japhet. Had it in fact been a bribe from him instead? I sat there for a long moment. It was time to confide in Bree.

I arrived at our modest off campus apartment a little after six. Traffic had been horrible on the highway, and an accident had only slowed things down even more. As I drove by the crumpled silver Ford Focus I was able to discern that it had Vermont plates. Bree and I had skied in Vermont a year before, a small place called Stowe that a friend had recommended to us. It did not really compare to Aspen or Boulder, but then, we had not exactly spent a lot of time on the slopes.

I knocked the early season mud off my shoes and opened the door. The tantalizing scent of Bree's famous pasta sauce greeted my nostrils, and Mozart played softly on the CD player.

"Babe? I'm home!"

She came through the kitchen archway with a black plastic spoon in one hand, and the other hand cupped beneath it. She grinned, "Try this," I opened my mouth obediently, "You got here just in time."

"Ha-ha. Heard it a thousand times. At least nine hundred from you." Everyone can make a good pasta sauce, but Bree takes it to the next level. I kissed her.

"How's your mom doing?" She asked.

I shrugged. "About as well as can be expected I guess. She doesn't seem to be in much pain." I removed my jacket and then Bree was in my arms.

"Love you."

"Love you too."

I followed her out into the kitchen where my sharp eyes noticed a pan of chocolate chip brownies as well. As I was reaching for them she smacked my knuckles sharply with the spoon.

"Hey! That hurt!"

"No brownies until after you eat."

I took her by the wrists and backed her up against the refrigerator and then kissed her mouth, cheek, and neck.

"If dinner burns, it's your fault."

"If dinner burns, we'll order take out." I let her go however, and chose a bottle of red wine to go with our meal.

Bree stood about shoulder height to my six foot frame, and it was obvious that she put her gym membership to good use. Her hair was a blond that did not come out of a bottle, and her eyes were a startling robin's egg blue. She was fair skinned and smiled easily. She made my life complete.

During dinner I struggled to find a way to share with her what I had learned today from my mother. I caught her studying me several times, between sips of wine or mouthfuls of food. She knew I wanted to tell her something, but instead of pressing, she was allowing me to find my own way of telling her.

At last I sighed and said, "My mother told me a great deal about her past. She—this is so hard to say! I can hardly believe it myself!"

Bree took my hand in hers. "Just tell me the truth, Justin. That can't be so hard."

"My mother claims she was rescued and then set free by modern day pirates. The leader of the pirates is my actual father. His name was—is, Erich Craigie." There, it was out. I could hardly believe it myself. It sounded so foolish and impossible. What would Bree think?

"I believe you, do you believe her?" Before I could jump to the defense of my mother, Bree continued, "Could this be a result of the medicine they have her on? Or a manifestation of something else?"

I shook me head. "I believed her, Bree." I took a sip of wine and tried to collect my thoughts. "It all makes sense, too. She also told me that Dad—Japhet, wants me to take over the business when he retires in a couple of years."

Bree frowned. "Is that what you want? I thought you were thinking about going into teaching?"

I nodded. "If I took over for Japhet, it would mean we would never have to worry about money for the rest of our lives."

"I'm not worried about money anyway. It's more important that you are happy. Would you be happy selling computers all day?"

"The only thing I'm truly sure of is that I want you in my life."

Her frown vanished and I squeezed her hand. I stared at one of the flickering candles she had placed on the table, and tried to figure out where to go from here with all of this.

"I support whatever you choose to do, Justin. You know that."

"Yeah, but I don't know what to do. I don't want to make my father angry, and there aren't any guarantees in teaching. It's a vicious Catch-22. You can't get a teaching job unless you have experience, and you can't get any experience unless you get a teaching job. Then, if I did find a position, with yearly budget cuts the standard practice now, there's no telling how long I would be able to teach until my job was cut."

"What about working for your father while you try and find a teaching job? That way, if it doesn't work out, at least you'll have something to fall back on. Maybe you could substitute teach as well, that would give you some experience as well as getting you known in the local schools."

"That's a good idea, but I'm not sure if my schedule would be flexible enough to allow me to sub, and work in the computer store. It also seems like a lot of people I have known over the years started out with a goal to do something, and then were side tracked into a job they ended up hating."

Bree looked into my eyes for a long moment. "Now you're just making excuses. If you want to teach, then do it. If you don't want to work in the computer store, then don't. You'd be a great teacher, Justin. I know you care about kids and how much you enjoyed your student teaching experience. You've also said you would like to coach and be involved in other after school activities. You're the type of person that will make a difference in kids' lives."

There was a long moment of silence between us, and then she changed the subject, "Why would your mother tell you all of this now? The whole pirate thing? I'm not asking in a negative way, but do you think she has an ulterior motive?"

I thought about that, and then ventured, "Maybe just to die with a clear conscience?"

"Maybe." Bree was not one to put words in someone else's mouth, and as usual, she was examining an issue from all angles before offering her opinion. It was one of her many traits which I admired.

"Do you think she wants me to try and find this Erich Craigie person, assuming he really does exist?" I suggested.

She shrugged, "I don't know. Is that what you're thinking?" It was my turn to raise my shoulders unknowingly. She continued, "I've seen some articles about modern day pirates, they're not exactly gregarious socialites, you know."

"It would be risky, yes. And it would have to wait until after graduation. That would give us a little time before we had to settle into careers."

"Us? We?"

"Of course. You don't think I would do this without you, do you? Besides, I would need someone to swab the decks and clean the fish."

"So our conversation went from career choices to you planning on trying to find your real father?" I nodded. "Gee, I'll have to check my social calendar. Sailing around the Caribbean with you sounds better than driving across the country, though."

"It wouldn't be the Caribbean, it's the Bermuda Triangle."

"I've heard of it. This isn't some weekend cruise you're talking about, you know. We'd have to hire a charter ship or something like that."

"That's what I was thinking. And the trip could be kind of like a pre-honeymoon for us."

Bree smiled in agreement, and then said, "There is only one sure way to find out what your mother is thinking."

"And that is?"

"Ask her."

I kissed my mother in greeting the next morning. Before I could even speak she said, "You must have so many questions, Justin, as well as doubts about what I have told you."

"Actually," I began, "I only really have one question. Why are you telling me about all of this—now?"

She answered without hesitation, "I wanted you to know the truth. I wanted someone to know the truth. What you do with this new knowledge is up to you. You're an adult now, and you deserve to know who your real father is. I'm not asking you to go on some wild goose chase to try and find Erich, although you may decide to try and find him."

"I wouldn't even know where to begin looking. The ocean is a big place."

She gave me a weak smile and changed the subject, "I remember when you were just a baby. You were a little roly-poly, always wriggling and chattering away. We did your baby room with an ocean theme. You would lie there and giggle and coo at the decorations—a sand dollar decal in particular fascinated you."

I grinned, not remembering any of this, but happy that she could.

"Your smile hasn't changed either. You always could light up a room with that ear to ear grin. Everybody who met you loved you. Even strangers would come up to me on the street and comment about what a beautiful baby you were. For your first Christmas we went to a photography studio and had your pictures done. You were dressed in a little Santa outfit and slept through the whole thing."

I had seen the pictures of this. To tell the truth, it was a bit embarrassing to remember that now. My mother and Japhet had used the picture as a Christmas card that year. A copy was in my baby book.

"Later that week, I took you in to sit on Santa's lap. He was so worried he would drop or hurt you. You were only a few months old at that time. Then came your first tooth, first haircut, potty training, first word, first step …" She sniffed and I handed her a Kleenex. "You grew up so fast, Justin. It seemed like one day I was putting a band aid on your knee from where you fell off your bike and the next day you were asking for the car keys to go on a date."

My first date I could remember. I was sixteen and as nervous as could be. Her name was Gwen, and she was the daughter of some family friends. Now that I thought back on it, I would not be surprised if our parents had been playing a little game of match maker. She had been attractive, but not exactly the brightest bulb in the box. I think we had gone out on at least one other occasion after that before I moved on to the next girl. For me, there had always been a next girl. Until Bree, that is.

I glanced down at my watch, "I've got to get going, Mom. I have class in a couple of hours." I was fortunate that the hospital my mother was in was close, not only to our apartment, but also to the university. I leaned over and kissed her cheek. "I'll be back tomorrow afternoon. You can regale me with more stories of my illustrious childhood."

She took my hand and squeezed it, "Goodbye, Justin."

Classes were the usual grind, especially now that spring was not that far off. People were more concerned with plans for Spring Break or post-graduation plans than listening to a professor's lecture. I had completed my student teaching internship in the fall. During that twelve week period under the supervision of the actual classroom teacher, I had taught four high school history classes. I had loved every minute of it. Although it had not been easy—in fact, I think I worked harder during those three months than I had the rest of my college career, I had learned a tremendous amount. I had also learned more during those three months in the classroom than I did in three years of college courses. Education classes were beneficial in theory, but there was not anything that could top actual experience.

There were myriad types of learning styles, as well as typical teenager issues. I was not much older than the students I was teaching, so I could relate to what was going on in their lives. It was during this time period that I also started to develop a discipline policy. I tried to treat everyone fairly, and expected them to treat me the way they wanted to be treated themselves. It had seemed to work.

It was a bit stressful on Bree's and my relationship. I spent a lot of time grading papers and assessments, and I also volunteered as an assistant to the Junior Varsity football team. Bree and I did not have exactly a lot of what one would call alone time. I would usually grade until about eleven, and then I was up at six and gone all day. Even weekends were spent on school related tasks or at football games.

The end of the internship was an emotional time for me. I had become attached to the students. They truly were a great bunch. They had a small party for me during class with a bunch of joke gifts including a plastic bat for discipline, a bottle of Aspirin for all the headaches, and a handful of red pens for grading. I had never used that color to grade, however. It brought back to many memories of themes which I had written which had come back looking like a small animal had bled to death on them. I was a bit embarrassed at the end of the day when my cooperating teacher confided in me that he knew for a fact of several of the female students who had crushes on me.

I had adamantly denied any fostering of those ideas, and assured him that I had maintained a professional distance from my students at all times. He had laughed and responded that he had not been implying any wrong doing on my part, but that it was something I needed to be aware of.

"You're a good-looking man, Justin. And as a teacher you will be in a position of power and trust. It's a sad truth that you will spend more time with your students than do their parents. It's a fact that some of your students will develop crushes on you. But never forget, you are a role model to them, and if you lose their trust, you won't ever be able to get it back."

That evening, while Bree was loading the dishwasher, I walked up behind her and wrapped my arms around her.

"I love you."

"I love you too. Give me a minute to finish this, will you?"

"No, Bree. I really love you."

She exhaled and turned to face me, brushing an errant strand of loose hair out of her face, "I really love you too, Justin. What are you going to do, ask me to marry you?"

This had long been a standing joke between us, and I had mock-proposed a half dozen times. I dropped down to one knee and looked up at her. From my back pocket I removed a blue felt jewelry box, and snapped it open. Inside was a three-quarter carat diamond flanked by two half quarter carat sapphires. Her eyes widened in surprise.

"Is that ... is ... are you—?"

"Bree? I can't promise you for richer, but I can promise for poorer. Will you marry me?"

She started laughing, thinking I was again joking. But I was not.

"Is that a yes or a no?"

Then she started crying.

"Um. Bree?"

"Yes, Justin. Yes, I'll marry you." She threw her arms around me and our mouths met. There was not anything else in the world that mattered during that moment in time.

Hours later, our arms and legs still tangled and dozing happily, the phone rang. I was immediately awake. Phone calls this time of night were either wrong numbers or bad news. I reached for the phone we kept beside the bed. It was one of the doctors from the hospital. I knew what he was going to say before he even continued after identifying himself. My mother was gone.

CHAPTER 2

▼

I did not cry at my mother's funeral. I know how cold that must sound, but I think it was a combination of shock, denial, and being overwhelmed. Empty condolences concerning how she was no longer in any pain, or that she had gone on to a better place offered little solace. Bree stood beside me the entire time, holding onto my hand tightly. Winter could not seem to make up its mind as to whether or not it wanted to stay or leave. We had received a couple inches of wet snow the night before, and now the sun was shining and had chased the snow away to the shadows.

I had trouble reconciling the fact that it was my mother who lay there in the coffin of dark mahogany wood. It just did not seem possible that she was dead. She had always been there for my entire life. Always vivacious and alive—so alive. I took a deep breath and Bree tightened her grip on my hand. The words of the priest whom I had never met before went in one of my ears and out the other. I had stopped believing in a God a long time ago, if in fact, I had ever truly believed. The empty consolations that everything happens for a reason, or that it was in the hands of a higher power and not for us to question, struck me as weak rationalizations in order to deal with pain and loss. To each their own, I guess.

They lowered my mother's body into the ground. More empty and meaningless words were said. I watched the entire process with an aloof detachment. Only when they started covering the casket with dirt did I turn away, not wishing to have to bear witness to that ordeal. When it was over, Bree and I left the cemetery hand in hand. Neither of us spoke as we found my car and got in. Sometimes, there are not any words. This was one of those times.

The next several days passed in a sort of gray fog. We both went back to our classes. After all, as the saying goes, life is for the living, and we had living to do. We were going to wait a year before we were married. Bree had already begun the planning part of the whole thing. Potential churches, florists, photographers, reception halls, caterers, and something called a videographer all went into a binder. She had even started drafting a guest list. I never realized I had that many relatives. A recently married friend confided in me that weddings are all about the women, and that it was best if the men just stayed out of the way.

I found myself in the microfiche section of the library one afternoon. Here one had access to the archived newspapers going back decades. On a whim, and because I had a couple of hours to kill before my next class, I decided to try and find any references to when my mother returned to civilization. I started with my birthday on October thirtieth, and began to work backward. Not finding anything, I scanned quickly back, and then I found it on August fourth.

Local Girl Returns Safe AP Press Cara Nichole Owens, presumed lost at sea in June of this year, was found safe yesterday afternoon by a routine Coast Guard patrol. Ms. Owens explained that the ship she had been sailing on with David Taylor III sank during a storm while they were on their way to the Atlantic Scientific Institute research center in Bermuda where they had internships. Ms. Owens was in remarkably good health. "I was able to survive on an island the last several months. I had fresh water from a nearby stream, and all the coconuts I could eat. I found a motorboat washed up on the beach, it still worked, and here I am." The parents of Ms. Owens were overjoyed at the return of their daughter. When asked what her future plans were, Mrs. Owens interjected, "She needs to recover from her ordeal." Ms. Owens is a recent graduate of Roger Williams University. Mr. David Taylor III is still missing and presumed lost at sea.

Not the best written article in the history of journalism, I thought. A few subject-verb agreement issues, several incomplete sentences, and at least one run-on sentence. Perhaps it had been a local or new reporter, or someone just in a hurry to meet a deadline. What really stood out was the fact that the article did not exactly coincide with what my mother had told me had happened.

I moved to a computer station and Googled David Taylor III. Affluent family, graduate of Roger Williams University, presumed lost at sea. I typed in Eric Craigy. The computer thought a moment before querying me did you mean Erich Craigie? I hit Enter and the similarities between Erich Craigie and David Taylor III were eerie. Affluent family, attended Exeter Academy, presumed lost at sea, also. Who puts all of this information into the computers anyway?

I returned to the newspaper archives. Someone called a hello to me and I waved without looking. A couple of days after the article about the miraculous return of my mother was a smaller article which I had missed during my initial scan.

David Taylor III Presumed Lost At Sea AP Press In light of the surprising return of Cara Nichole Owens earlier this week, the family of David Taylor III are not counting on a similar miracle for their son who was also onboard the ill-fated vessel. "Ms. Owens reported to authorities that our son was swept overboard by an errant wave. He gave his life to save hers, and only through his heroic actions was she eventually able to get to safety," said David Taylor II. "We have already mourned his loss, and to commemorate his life, the new weight room at Roger Williams University is being named in his honor, so that other athletes, like himself, will be able to succeed on and off the field."

I checked for a by-line to see if it was the same hack author who had written both articles. One of my professors in college used to complain that on line slang, cell phones, and text messages had contributed to the overall decline of the spoken and written English language. I added inept newspaper writers to the list.

The article went on to explain how David Taylor III had loved sports, and had played football, hockey, and lacrosse. My eyes widened in surprise as I read that fact. But then, those are the glory sports in high school and college. The article also implied without directly saying so that David Taylor II had donated the money to pay for the weight room named in his son's honor.

Back to the computer, I did a search for pirates and piracy. I spent the next hour learning about a history lesson I will not soon forget. At one time, all of North and South America had been claimed by Spain. This vast, unsettled area was known as The Spanish Main. To prepare for colonization, Spanish ships had unloaded cows and pigs on many of the islands and then allowed nature to take its course. The herds of animals, finding ample food and a safe environment, thrived. Other adventurers and explorers traveled to these islands, and found abundant food. To survive the boat trips between islands, they dried the meat from the animals on wooden racks called boucans. These early explorers became known as Boucaneers, and then later as buccaneers.

The British wanted some of this rich land for their own. In the sixteen hundreds they attacked the Spanish settlement of Santa Domingo and were soundly defeated. As they retreated they raided and captured Jamaica. The British hired the buccaneers as mercenaries to not only protect Jamaica, but to harass the Spanish, as well. This kept Spain occupied with other concerns, and the English were free to expand in the new world.

Many of these buccaneers went on to become Privateers. These Privateers, or pirates, were still mainly mercenaries for the British, and fought mostly for money. The main difference between a Privateer and a buccaneer was that the Privateers owned their own ships. They would raid the commercial or supply ships of the Spanish, and then split the captured cargo with the British. Privateers were also required to register their ships and actions, as well as getting a license to practice privateering.

The most famous of all of these British Privateers was Henry Morgan. In the sixteen sixties he was named admiral of all the privateers and buccaneers. Soon after, he raided Portobelo which at that time was the third largest Spanish port in the Spanish Main. Despite being heavily defended, Admiral Morgan and his men took Portobelo. This caused a great deal of fear among the Spanish, because if Portobelo were not safe, there was not any Spanish stronghold that was.

In sixteen hundred and seventy-one, Morgan attacked and captured Panama which was the second largest port and city in the new world, and the wealthiest. However, historical texts suggested that much of Panama's wealth and art were snuck out of the city even as Morgan was attacking it. There are some historians who think Morgan stole much of the missing money and treasure, yet records indicate that pirates burying their ill-gotten gains is just a popular myth fostered by fictional works of literature and movie sensationalism. Contrary to popular belief, there are not any treasure maps. An authentic pirate treasure map has never been found. Typical pirates would raid either settlements or other ships, and if successful, would then spend the money on women, debauchery, and rum. Not necessarily in that order. Then they would start the entire process all over again.

In sixteen hundred and seventy-two, King Charles the Second summoned Morgan to England, knighted him, and appointed him Lieutenant Governor of Jamaica. Henry Morgan lived the rest of his life uneventfully until his death in sixteen eighty-eight.

I glanced at my watch and saw I was going to be late for my class if I did not get going. But I was a history major, and this was historical research that I was doing. I went back to reading from the web pages that I had called up. The internet is a wonderful thing sometimes.

The Queen Anne's War of seventeen hundred and one lasted thirteen years with Holland and England on one side, and France and Spain on the other. When the war ended, a treaty was signed that allowed free trade throughout the area formerly known as The Spanish Main. More importantly, the Privateers were not needed any longer. It became illegal to raid any ship—a law if broken was punishable by death. Literally thousands of Privateers were suddenly and unexpectedly out of work.

In seventeen seventeen, Edward Teach and a small group of former Privateers attacked the British ship Concord and captured her. They renamed the ship Queen Anne's Revenge after the war which had recently ended. They armed her with forty cannons which at the time made her one of the largest and most formidable pirate ships on the water.

During the next eighteen years Edward Teach gathered over four hundred other pirates and a small fleet of ships, and wreaked havoc on the seas. It was during this time that he became known by his more famous name of Blackbeard.

In seventeen eighteen all pirates and Privateers were given full governmental pardons absolving them of all prior crimes against humanity only if they renounced piracy. Blackbeard instead blockaded Charles Towne, South Carolina, and did not allow any ship to enter or leave the harbor. A group of dignitaries rowed out to try and reason with him, and were instead captured and held for exorbitant ransoms.

Blackbeard soon became the most hunted pirate on the seas, and later that year, during a sword fight with a British captain on a ship he and his crew were raiding, Blackbeard was struck in the neck and throat from behind and died almost immediately.

While Blackbeard was the most famous or infamous pirate of this era, there were many others listed as well. Black Bart Roberts raided over four hundred ships in a three year period. There were many other pirates as well, and I was shocked to read of the mayhem they had caused. There were even female pirates who had been just as bloodthirsty!

I scrolled down and the pirate references continued, but they were all from about the same time period. I went back to the top and typed in a search for modern-day pirates without much hope of finding anything substantial. Imagine my surprise when I was again greeted with a lengthy list. One of the most recent attacks had been on a cruise ship. While the pirates had used rocket launchers and machine guns, they had never actually boarded the ship, but the passengers had been understandably shaken up.

That had been in two thousand and five. The Seaborn Spirit had been cruising off the African Coast, authorities had been confident that the attackers were Somalian pirates. The year before, over thirty people had been killed in confirmed acts of piracy. This did not include a lengthy list of missing people and property. How many others had died at the hands of pirates was unknown. There had been a hundred and six reported cases of piracy in nineteen ninety-two. That number had jumped in under ten years to over three hundred and seventy confirmed incidents of pirate activity! As a student of history the numbers alone were staggering! Reported pirate incidents in two thousand and two had included over a hundred cases alone in Indonesia. Thirty plus more attacks had occurred in Bangladesh, and scattered accounts across the world of other attacks, as well.

The sun had moved to the opposite wall as I returned to the top of the search page and typed in a search for the Bermuda Triangle. The history lesson continued. The most commonly assumed points of the Bermuda or Devil's Triangle were composed of Bermuda, Puerto Rico, and Miami, Florida. This encompassed over a million and a half miles of land and water. Another common name for the area was the Triangle of Death. How pleasant, I thought, scratching behind my ear as I tried to digest all of this information.

The Bermuda Triangle, however, was a misnomer. Many charts also considered the entire eastern coast of Florida, Georgia, and South Carolina, as part of the 'cursed' area. Instead of a triangle it made more of a lopsided rectangle. It had earned its most popular moniker in nineteen sixty-four, although the most famous incident involving the area had happened over twenty years before it earned its official name.

Twenty years before it became known as the Bermuda Triangle, on a routine training mission, five Navy torpedo planes called Avengers were supposed to make a practice bombing run on Bimini. Flight Nineteen had vanished, as did the search plane that went out looking for them.

The Avengers were sturdy planes, which is why the Navy used them, and it was assumed that some type of wreckage would be found. The Avengers were well known for their buoyancy, and ir was assumed that some trace of their whereabouts would be located.

There was never any evidence of Flight Nineteen nor their demise found. Many theories existed about what may have happened, but there was never any conclusive proof located. During the nineteen eighties alone, over thirty-five planes vanished in the area. These aircraft were never located, as well.

The area in which the Bermuda triangle encompassed was notorious for unpredictable storms and currents. Due to some of the deep sea trenches in the area, water depths could vary quickly from barely covered shoals and sandbars, to water depths of several hundred feet or more. These water depths also contributed to erratic and freak 'Rogue' waves in the area. Navigation was often difficult because compasses would point to true north instead of magnetic north. This could change the course of a ship or plane by many miles. Had my mother become lost? She had said they were caught in a storm, so it was almost a certainty that they had been blown off their original course.

I sighed, closed out of the page, and logged off. Lots of interesting facts to be sure, but they were just leading me to more questions. How would I find my real father in over a million miles of water? Would he want to be found? How would he react if and when we did meet? Just how much danger was I putting myself, and more importantly, Bree, into?

Lacing my fingers behind my head I arched my back and listened to the vertebrae pop and crack. It was a bad habit of mine, and drove Bree crazy. I still had so many questions about all of this. Then I leaned forward. Grandmother Owens lived a couple of hours away in York, Pennsylvania. Perhaps she would have some answers for me. My mother had returned home and stayed with my grandmother for a while before she had met Japhet. I was hoping she would be able to provide some of the proverbial further light on the subject.

The trip up the Pennsylvania Turnpike was uneventful, and tedious. You would think that a five-laned highway would move along smoothly, but not in this case. I took the exit to York, and drove down several side streets before arriving at my grandmother's modest house. I was unsure how she would receive my unannounced visit, but as we had always gotten along well in the past, I was not overly concerned.

I gave a gentle knock on the storm door and waited in as patient a manner as I could. Moments later, my grandmother peered through a side window and then opened the front door wide. "Justin Allen! How nice to see you!"

"Hello, Grandmother," I replied with an inward sigh of relief.

She was the stereotypical grandmother: short, a cloud of white hair, whip-thin, and doting on her grandchild. There were some extra lines in her face since my mother's death, and her smile did not quite reach her eyes as I had remembered it doing in the past.

"Come in, come in," she beckoned, and I entered the house. It was not exactly dark, but it was not bright either. My grandmother seemed to exist in an eerie twilight regardless of the time of year or the weather outside. Her house had always reminded me of a museum with the antique furniture, hard covered books, bric-a-brac, and souvenirs of her travels. Everything looked like it had not been touched in a thousand years. A beep came from the kitchen.

"Excuse me while I go pull those cookies from the oven."

Why are grandmothers always cooking? Who was I to complain when I was about to be the beneficiary of said cooking? I followed her out into the kitchen. She had a nervous energy about her, whether she had always been like that or because it was a result of losing not only a husband, but also a daughter in less then five years, I was unsure. I sat down at the same wooden table I remembered her having from when I was a young child.

I used to sit at that heavy solid maple table and color or draw for hours. Sometimes I would make up stories to go along with the pictures. Both my mother and grandmother would ooh and ahh over my creation of the moment, and then it would find a place of honor on the refrigerator. I learned to write in cursive copying from my mother's handwriting at that table. I followed the patterns of the letters, not able to read what I was writing. Later, in high school, and sometimes even in college, I would sit at that table and do my homework, sometimes with pen and paper, more recently on a lap top.

"Tea?" She inquired, ever the gracious hostess, and I nodded. "Thank you so much for the invitation to your graduation, but I'm not sure I'll be able to make it."

I nodded, not really listening. She continued, "We're having a big art show that weekend, and I'm afraid I won't be able to get away." My grandmother was on the board of directors at the Strand-Capitol Performing Arts Center.

I flipped through the York Daily Record to see what was going on in the world, or at least in this part of it. She also subscribed to the York Dispatch, figuring that between the two newspapers there would hopefully be some accuracies. A magnet on the refrigerator that proudly proclaimed "I ride the Rabbit," caught my eye. Rabbit Transit was the major transportation company in this city most famous for the York Peppermint Patty. York was not overly large, only about forty thousand people lived here. Yet it was also a city that served as host for a barbell factory, a Harley-Davidson factory, and the regional headquarters for Starbucks and Bon-Ton.

She poured the tea and sat down across from me. "You're very quiet today, Justin Allen." My grandmother was notorious for including middle names when addressing someone.

I shrugged. "I'm still trying to come to terms with my mother dying."

"Of course, of course. Aren't we all." It was not a question, just a resigned statement of a fact on her part. We were all suffering, and I was ashamed of my selfishness.

I sighed, and asked, "Did she ever mention anything about when she was shipwrecked?"

My grandmother frowned in thought. She nibbled at her bottom lip pensively, a habit that my mother and I also shared. "That was over twenty years ago, but I remember it about tore the family apart at the thought of losing her. She had an internship at the Atlantic Scientific Institute and Research Center in Bermuda. She and a male classmate," here she frowned in disapproval, "Decided to sail there instead of flying. I would have paid her airfare, but I think she was too proud to ask. I should have insisted. If only she had flown ..."

I nodded. If only she had flown. If she had gone by plane I probably would not be sitting here right now, and who knows what would have happened, how things would have worked out?

"If I remember correctly, they were about half way there when they were caught in a severe tropical storm. The boat sank. Cara Nichole said she remembered waking up on a beach. She said she looked for the boy but his body was never recovered." She took a deep breath, "We turned that ocean upside down looking for her—them. The authorities looked for three weeks before calling off the search. When the authorities had given up hope, I hired people to continue looking for her. They never found a trace, it was if they had vanished. I never gave up that she was still alive though." She looked into my eyes. "I never gave up and my faith was rewarded. The Coast Guard found her floating in a rowboat that she had found washed up on shore."

I nodded. Despite a few extra facts, this was similar to the story my mother had told me she had presented to the world. Would anyone have believed the truth? I was not sure I would.

"I'm forgetting something …" My grandmother frowned in consternation, and then sharply snapped her fingers. "Oh, yes! Your mother left some things for you!"

"Things?" I replied, confused. But she had bustled off bird-like into one of the guest rooms. I heard her mumbling to herself, and desk drawers opening and sliding shut, and then silence. She reappeared with a triumphant smile on her face.

"I guess I'm not that far gone, yet."

She placed a faded brown papered box in front of me. It was roughly twice the size of a case of CDs or DVDs. When she slid it across the table to me there was a slight shifting noise from inside. It sounded like a whisper of a promise to answer some of my questions.

"What is it?"

She shrugged. "Cara Nichole made me promise to give you this before she went into the hospital—for the last time. I don't know what's in it, but she was earnest about you getting it."

"I wonder why she didn't just give it to me herself?"

I opened up the box and inside were a dozen or so delicate, top-shaped shells. Some were cracked, chipped, or broken, but several were whole. There was also a note. I opened the paper and read in my mother's neat, no-nonsense handwriting, a letter dated a month before her death.

"My dearest Justin, if you are reading this, then I have passed on, and we have also had our talk about who your real father was. He gave me these shells off a beach near his camp. They are Turnip Whelks and are normally only found in the Gulf of Mexico. If you do go to Bermuda to search for him, check

the beaches of islands along the way. If you find shells similar to these, you'll know you're in the right place. I am so sorry for leaving you without a mother, Justin. But I am so very proud of you. Giving birth to you was the best thing I ever did. I wish only the best for you and Brianna. No mother could ask for a better daughter-in law, and certainly not for a better son. I will always be with you. Love, your mother."

I wiped at the tears in my eyes and snuffled loudly. My grandmother passed me a tissue.

"What did the note say?"

I picked up one of the shells that looked like rolled ribbon candy. It was round on top and tapered to a long point on one end. There were brown and maroon horizontal stripes down its sides. I looked up at my grandmother and answered her question as well as my own,

"Everything."

CHAPTER 3

▼

I've always loved the sound of bagpipes. Their haunting melody calls to an ancient and dark part of my soul. I sat on a hard, gun-metal gray folding chair at graduation, beneath a blazing sun, and looked around into a sea of faces. My grandmother, true to her word, had not been able to make it due to prior commitments, and of course my mother was not there for obvious reasons. Japhet was too occupied with his business. I was utterly alone. Despite being surrounded by several hundred classmates, I had never felt more alone in my entire life.

I reflectively examined these feelings of isolation. I had never been truly alone before. Growing up I had been surrounded by friends and family, and this had continued into college. Meeting Bree had been the best thing that had ever happened to me, yet committing to her had done little to impact my social life. I still hung out with male friends, played intramural sports, and so on. We were both gregarious and outgoing, and maintained large groups of personal and collective friends.

She sat about fifteen rows ahead of me, wearing the same nerdy mortarboard hat and school colored gown. While I had several friends in my vicinity, one of whom was passing around a bottle of tequila, I had never felt more alone in my life. College graduation is a lot of things, I thought. Mostly it is an ending. It is the end of true youth and irresponsibility, and the brink of adulthood, maturity, and responsibility. I was not entirely sure I was ready for it.

I had interviewed for several teaching positions, but only half-heartedly. Japhet had intoned on several occasions that there was a management position open at any store I wanted if the "teaching thing" as he put it, did not work out. He also understood that I would be spending the first several weeks of the summer on a sailing trip. He did not like it, but I was an adult now, after all. I had explained that I needed a break from school, and that it was a sort of a trial or mini-honeymoon for Bree and me.

"You go to school for four years with summers off, a month long Christmas break, and you still need time off?" He had said in his blustery voice that always reminded me of a car with a bad exhaust system trying to get started on a cold day. "I don't get time off like that. You better hope this," teaching thing, I inserted silently before he could say it, "teaching thing pays off, because you'll never get that much time off in the real world."

"Yes, sir." I had replied. Japhet had been in the Marine Corps. During my late teens he had pushed for me to join up as well. Not that I'm a coward, but that was also about the time the whole mess in Iraq and Afghanistan had been going down. No thank you.

"It'll make a man out of you," he had said in regards to the military. "Give you some valuable life experiences, instead of spending all of your time reading books." More like give me prosthetic limbs—if I were lucky and survived the IED with my name on it. "Battle experience looks good on a resume, as well. It shows you can be a leader of men. If you're going to run my company someday, your employees will respect you for it." Even then I was not sure that I wanted to run his company. I was not as wise then and had ventured,

"I'm not sure I want to run Thyme Computers ..."

His face had turned red but that had been the end of the conversation. After my mother's death he and I had for the most part avoided each other. We had been like two old caged lions, endlessly circling, and circling.

I did not really listen to any of the graduation speakers. I remembered listening intently to the people who spoke at my high school commencement, and despite it only being four years earlier, I could not recall a single word any of them had said. I wondered if that were true for everyone, or if it was just a mix of excitement and trepidation on my part. Today, perhaps, it could also have been the tequila.

The speakers finally finished and sat down. Others stood up and took their places. The sun grew hotter, and at last they began calling the names of the graduates. One by one graduates took their solitary walk up to the stage, shook hands with various dignitaries, received their diploma, and then walked back to their seat, even as the next person had been called and was shaking hands. To me it had all the solemnity of a prisoner being marched off to his death sentence. For in the end, we all made that walk alone.

The announcer spoke Bree's name. I clapped loudly as she regally made her way up to the podium. Behind me there was a loud cheer from what I assumed were her family and friends. Bree's family had been very accepting of me from the very first time we met, and I got along with all of them quite well, also. They liked to tease her fourteen year old sister Kathy, who they assured me had a huge crush on me.

More names, more clapping and cheers. People I had spent four years with, some on an almost daily basis. I wondered for a brief moment if I would ever see most of them again, and the cynic in me that had raised his ugly head on this supposed to be joyous day doubted it. I knew that things could not stay the same, but it was so difficult to come to terms with. Plus c'est la meme chose, plus ca change, or if you are a purist, le plus de choses change, le plus ils restent pareil.

"Justin. Allen. Thyme." The announcer soomoned. I stood and methodically made my way toward the podium. I was aware of people applauding, and some camera flashes. I focused on not tripping over my graduation robes and making a fool of myself in front of everyone.

"Congratulations," said the president of the university. A word he would repeat several hundred times that day. Perhaps that was why he spoke without conviction or emotion in his voice. Even his handshake was dry and quick. Pump, pump, pump, release. I moved on, received my diploma, and wended my way back to my seat.

After the official ceremony, we had some friends over to our apartment for a small celebration. Bottles of champagne were opened, toasts were made, and there were lots of hugs and kisses going around. Empty promises to stay in touch were made, but the truth was, we were all about to be dispersed randomly into the world. I attempted to find a happy celebratory spot in myself to share, but was unable to do so. Everyone was discussing their plans that a week ago and been referred to in the future tense, but were now becoming the present. Internships, travel plans, careers, and Bree and I were not the only ones planning weddings.

In the midst of all this reverie, with the facade of a smile pasted to my face, I noticed a sensible, navy blue BMW pull into our crowded driveway. Japhet slowly got out of the car. He surveyed the other vehicles with a critical eye, observed the dozen or so people mingling on our modest front lawn, and at last made eye contact with me. He nodded in greeting, and then walked over to where I was standing. He extended his right hand and we shook.

"Congratulations, son." He used the same tone as the president had earlier in the day.

"Thank you, Sir. Thank you for driving all this way to see us."

He nodded. Japhet had also grown some extra lines around his eyes and face since the death of my mother. I was again reminded, just as I had been with my grandmother, that I was not the only one still mourning her death. Japhet was somewhat overweight, and his asthma often caused him to wheeze. The man I had assumed for over twenty years to be my father was mostly bald, and wore bifocals. His face was red from walking the thirty yards from his car to me. We stood staring at each other, neither knowing what to say next.

"Dad!" Bree came over carrying a full glass of champagne. It might have been my imagination, but I thought he cringed at her greeting. She hugged him while he stood there stiffly. Japhet had never been the type to show much emotion or affection. He also had not cried at my mother's funeral.

"Champagne?" Bree offered him the glass she was holding, but he shook his head and declined. Japhet was more of a scotch and soda man, or wine when celebrating.

"No, thank you." He thought a moment, "I will take a glass of red wine, if you have it?"

"Of course!" Bree hastened off to get the wine for Japhet.

"I can't stay long, Son. Business, you know. But I wanted to give you this in person." He reached inside the left breast pocket of his sports coat and removed an envelope. "This should cover your trip plus expenses for the next couple of weeks."

I thumbed open the envelope and was surprised to find a thick row of crisp one hundred dollar bills.

"Thank you. I …"

He held up a hand stopping me. "No need to thank me, Son. Your mother … your mother always loved the ocean. Just please come home safe. I don't think I could stand losing—losing both of you." He fought back a coughing fit, but he had tears in his eyes. I embraced him. Japhet was the only father I had ever really known, and he had provided well for my mother and me. Was I doing the right thing by going on this trip? I fought back the guilty feeling and second thoughts I was having about leaving. He stepped back from my embrace.

"I have to get going now. Business, you know."

I nodded. It had always been business, you know. He started to turn away.

"But Bree is bringing you some wine. And don't you want to say good-bye to her?" as if either really mattered to him. He did pause, and rubbed at the graying stubble along his jaw.

"Another time perhaps. Don't forget, when you get back, if the teaching thing doesn't work out, you will always have a place waiting for you in the family company."

"Thank you." I held up the envelope. "Thank you again." He waved off my words dismissively, as if shooing flies. I watched him walk back down to his car, get in, and drive off. Bree returned moments later carrying a glass of red wine.

"Where did your father go? Is he still here?"

"He left." I was unable to keep the sigh of disappointment out of my voice. "Business, you know."

She nodded toward the envelope. "Is that your graduation present?"

I grinned, unable to contain my excitement and happiness. Using a forefinger and thumb, I opened the envelope to show her the contents. Her eyes grew wide. "This should cover our trip."

"Oh, Justin!" She threw her arms around me and hugged me tight. Paying for our vacation had been a bit of a concern for us both. While we both had some money saved up, most of it had been earmarked to pay for our wedding, which was really starting to add up. Maybe I should have majored in photography, or flowers, or catering. You get the idea.

"Hey, don't spill the wine! It's over twenty dollars a bottle!" But she just laughed and kissed me again, and of course we spilled the wine.

The party continued on into the wee hours of the morning. It finally broke up around three. After receiving Japhet's monetary gift, I was in a much more jovial mood. It was if a large weight had been lifted from my shoulders. After the last guest had left I locked our front door and turned off the porch light. Bree was occupied with attempting to clean up the living room. I went over and lifted her into my arms.

"Hey! I wanted to get this cleaned up tonight—I mean this morning."

"It can wait." I kissed her and carried her into our bedroom.

I awoke the next morning to the scent of coffee brewing and bacon frying. I stretched, pulled on a pair of scrub pants someone had given me, and made my way into the kitchen where Bree was wearing a blue terry-cloth robe and busy making breakfast.

"Morning, Love." I kissed her on back of the neck.

"Good morning. Two or four pieces of toast with your eggs?"

"Two, please." I poured us each a mug of coffee, added sugar and cream, and then sat down, reaching for the morning newspaper.

"Um-mm." She interrupted. "You're up, so you're in charge of the toast."

"Ah, putting all of my vast repertoire of culinary skills to use. How about I do the dishes instead?"

She paused, considering my proposal. "And take out the garbage?"

"Don't I always?" She rolled her eyes. "Don't I usually?" I amended.

"Is this what married life with you is going to be like?"

"Well, yeah. That and the six kids we're going to have running around."

"Six!" Her eyes widened. "Here's a deal for you then, I'll have the first two if you have the last four!"

Chuckling, I stood and brought the three bags of garbage left over from our party out to the curb for morning pick up. Bree meanwhile finished making breakfast. I went back into the kitchen, washed my hands, and we sat down to eat.

As we were eating and I was flipping through the morning section of sports, Bree asked, "So, what's the plan?"

I swallowed a piece of toast and washed it down with some coffee before answering, "I was thinking of chartering a sailboat and hiring someone who knows his way around the area. We could probably sail out of Charleston without too much of a problem. I figure we'll sail for three or four weeks, depending on cost, come home, finish planning our wedding, get married, and start careers."

"Sounds like a good plan. Anything else?"

I stood up and leaned over to hug her before adding, "And live happily ever after."

"Definitely a good plan. What exactly are you hoping to find out in the ocean?"

"More answers. Maybe my real father."

"It's a big ocean, Justin."

"Yes, it is." I then proceeded to share with her the letter from my mother, as well as the information about the box of seashells.

"Well," she said, "it's still going to be like looking for a needle in a haystack."

"More like a specific needle in a stack of needles."

"When were you thinking of leaving on this trip?"

"Well," I paused in thought, "it will probably take at least a couple of weeks to get our finances in order. Plus another week to charter a boat and captain. How does leaving around the second week in June sound to you?"

Bree nodded. "Sounds good. Are we going to follow the original course your mother's ship was on?"

"That's what I was thinking. We'll probably meander around a bit as well. As I said before, I'm hoping this will be sort of a mini-vacation for us. We haven't had a lot of just-the-two-of-us time lately."

The next few weeks passed quickly, probably because we were both so busy preparing for our upcoming trip. Our time was consumed with planning, preparation, packing, and putting our affairs in order. Knowing we might be encountering some dangerous situations, I drove out of the city to visit RJ Bushey, an old high school friend who now owned a sporting goods store.

He greeted me in a warm manner as I entered his bright and clean store. "Justin Thyme!" He clapped me hard on the shoulder. "Long time, no see! How have you been?"

We shook hands and made some small talk, catching up. Although we had seldom seen each other since graduation, we had played starting attack together on our high school lacrosse team. It surprised me that in just four years he had put on some weight and was definitely showing some signs of premature balding.

"I'm doing well, RJ. I just graduated from Maryland University ..."

"Heckuva lacrosse team they've got! Didja play for them?"

"No, I was never that good. A little intramural ball, though. I'm engaged to a wonderful girl ..."

"Hey, congrats, man! Marriage ain't all it's cracked up to be, though. You remember Donna Stacey?"

I nodded, but could not really put a face with the name. She had been an underclassman.

"Well, she and I tied the knot a coupla years ago. Had a little boy—Junior, ya know."

"Well, congratulations to you, then!" RJ did not strike me as the fatherly type, however.

"Nah." He waved his hands, reminding me of how Japhet had done the same thing when I tried to thank him for the money. "We've been separated now for about eight months. Hey, ya know why wedding dresses are all white?"

I shrugged, not sure where this was going.

"So they'll match the 'frigerator and washing machine!" He cackled loudly, but without real humor. I was starting to recall why we had stopped spending time together.

"Hey, 'member that time against South Middleton, and I scored five goals?"

I nodded dumbly again. I was not sure if he had ever scored more than two goals in a game against a quality opponent, let alone five against our biggest rival. Trevor Quince had always been our big scorer on attack.

"Yeah, you and ol' Trev couldn't do squat that day, so it was up to me to carry the team, yet again. So, hey, what brings you to my humble little establishment anyway?"

It was hardly humble, but it did not sound like RJ's ego needed any more stroking than he had already given it. "My fiancee and I are taking a little sailing trip, and I've heard it can be rough out on the water." He gave me a blank look, not understanding. "I'd like a little added insurance, if you will, in case anyone gives us a hard time while we're on board the boat."

"Oh, yeah, man. You sure you want to go out on the ocean after what happened to your mom?" My mother's experiences as she had explained them were common knowledge in the area. The joys of living in a small town.

"Yeah, I'm sure. I was hoping you would be able to point me," I paused to see if he got the pun, but he did not, no surprise, really. "in the right direction regarding some guns that are good for self defense?"

Smelling a sale, as all good retailers are able to do, his attitude changed at once. "Of course, of course! Follow me." And just like that, the painful topic of my mother was dropped. I wondered if he knew that she had died. I did not think so. RJ lived in his own little myopic world, of guns and made up lacrosse statistics where he was always the hero. We stopped in front of a solid looking case with a glass top. With a small silver key he opened it up and removed several cases holding pistols, and placed them in a reverential manner on the table.

"Now this one," he lifted a compact-looking matte-black pistol, "is a Glock 22 9 millimeter. It's a forty caliber and has a lot of knock down power. A lot of cops and military types carry these." He sighted down the barrel and pointed at a far wall. "Ka-pow!" He shouted, and a pimply sales clerk jumped. He turned, and pushed the weapon toward me, handle first. It felt solid in my hand, and I nodded. He continued his prattling,

"It's a compact, solid weapon, just what you're looking for. It holds fifteen rounds and is a semi-automatic. That means it will go through a clip as fast as you can pull the trigger. It's a simple, but reliable gun, invented by an Austrian named Gaston Glock back in the early sixties."

I nodded again. It felt good in my hand. Right. Powerful. As if it belonged there. Using my left hand, I cupped my right as I had seen on TV, and sighted down the barrel.

"Aw, no need for that Justin. The Glock is light and there's hardly any recoil or kick. Only the cops do that," he nodded toward my pose. "Only the ones on TV, anyway. Say, you wanna squeeze off a few rounds with it?"

"Sure." I held up a hand to prevent him from scurrying off just yet. "But I'm also looking for—I guess an assault rifle? Like an M-16?"

His eyes widened and so did his grin. "I got something even better. You watch the news much? C-Span? CNN?" Before I could answer his rhetorical questions, he gestured for me to follow him to the back of the store. Once there we stood before a wall of deadly looking rifles. He genuflected before his jingoistic shrine, as devout as any holy man.

RJ reached up and took one of the assault rifles down off the wall. "This little beauty is an M-4. It's a shorter, lighter version of the M-16 A2. Although almost eighty percent of the parts are similar, it's gas operated, air-cooled, and has a telescoping stock with three different length settings." It felt almost as if he were trying to sell me a car, running through all of the features and perks that did not make a whole lot of sense to most people. Bottom line, maybe that was all RJ really was, a slick, oily, used car salesman. He was still rambling away.

"It's a 45 millimeter, and can shoot twenty to thirty rounds on single, semi, or three round burst. That means every time you pull the trigger, three shells come out. I can't sell you a fully automatic—well, I could, but it's illegal." He grinned. "Or you can just take out the firing pin and that'll make her fully automatic too. Best of all, it's good in close quarters. The military use these, so you've probably seen them on TV."

I interrupted his sales speech, "I'll take them. I'll take both of them."

"You will?" He seemed surprised. "I mean, of course you will! You wanted to squeeze off a few rounds as well, right?"

"Right." He grabbed several boxes of ammunition off a shelf, two pairs of ear protectors, and gestured for me to follow him through a side door which lead past his office and to an indoor shooting range.

"You want bull's-eye or human silhouette?"

"The silhouettes." I replied without hesitation. He eyed me with a confused look on his face. We spent the next half hour loading, unloading, and sighting in the pistol and rifle at several different distances. At first I aimed for the head area of the targets, but RJ admonished me, "Aim for the body. The head is too risky, too small of a target. Either one of these will knock a man down if you can hit him." I wondered for a moment if I would be able to point a gun at another human and pull the trigger. If it were a matter of protecting Bree or not, I did not have the faintest doubt that I would be able to squeeze the trigger. The lesson ended with RJ showing me how to break down and clean both of the guns.

Back in the store he paused and whispered in a conspiratorial voice, "Normally I'd hafta make you wait a couple of weeks before you could pick them up. Background checks and paperwork you understand. Today's what, Wednesday? Tell ya what, swing by Saturday and you'll be good to go. I'll throw in a couple boxes of shells for you as well."

Shells. He meant bullets, or rounds, or whatever the correct term for them was. For some odd reason I was reminded of the box of Turnip Whelk shells my mother had left for me. All of these strange connections between things that were not really connected at all. Or were they? It made me dizzy thinking about it. It was similar to contemplating the size of the universe.

He rang me up and when I saw the total, I cringed. That is what credit cards are for. We shook hands and I started walking toward the front door, congratulating myself on the ease with which I had handled the entire process. These were the first guns I had ever bought, or owned for that matter. As I was opening the door RJ's voice caused me to pause.

"Justin?" I turned back into the store and raised my eyebrows. He poked the inside of his left cheek with his tongue, trying to find the words. "I could put laser sights on both of those for ya, for a little extra, of course."

"No thanks, RJ. I still need to figure out how to explain this to my fiancee."

He laughed without humor. "You guys planning on having kids?" I nodded. "Let me tell ya somethin' about babies … it's a lie that all they do is sleep. Oh, they do sleep once in a while, but the rest of the time all they do is scream. It wears on a man, ya know?"

I reached out and grasped the handle of the door again, escape was that close. His next sentence came out in a rush of words, "We should hang out sometime, talk about the old days, the glory days!"

I could not bear the look on his pathetic face. "Sure, RJ. Sure. Maybe when we get back from our trip. I'll see you on Saturday. Around noon?" He nodded and I stepped out into the street and took a deep breath. I tried to muster up some sympathy for him. He was only twenty-two, and already had a failed marriage and a child. True, he had his own business, but that was all he ever would have, and he would be lucky if he was able to keep it. Which left him always wanting to relive twisted glory days that had not happened all that long ago. What would he be like at thirty? Forty? Fifty? Was that similar to my fate if I did not teach and instead took over Japhet's computer business? I got into my BMW and drove home for an uncertain confrontation with Bree.

"You did what?" I had never seen Bree so angry before. We never really argued about anything, and as for raising our voices in disagreement? Never. I mean, there are rough spots in all relationships, for instance, I hated her immense shoe collection scattered around the house, and my blowing my nose in the shower absolutely disgusted her, even though it washed down the drain. But as far as angry enough to yell? Never. Until now.

"Hon, I bought two guns for our trip," I repeated. I had said it in a light tone of voice after coming home and kissing her, and then she had launched into her tirade. I attempted to placate her further, "A pistol and a rifle ... for protection."

I guess it had been a rhetorical question with an answer that did not need repeating. Bree shook her head in angry denial, her mouth a tight line. "Don't you 'Hon,' me. I hate guns."

"Bree, if we run into any—trouble out there, I want to be able to protect you."

"Protect me? Protect me? If it's going to be so dangerous that you have to go and buy not one but two guns, maybe we should think twice about going on this trip in the first place!"

"I could not argue with that logic, but I tried. "Look, Bree ..."

"Don't 'look, Bree,' me! I hate guns. I hate them. You know about my cousin ..."

Indeed I did. Although I had never met him, I knew the story well. If you date someone long enough, you end up being privy to all kinds of stories. Some of them you are better off not knowing about. Bree's cousin Joseph had shot himself in the head when he was sixteen. He had not left a note or ever told anyone anything before he had decided to pull the trigger.

I exhaled. "I'm not going to lie to you. It can be dangerous out on the ocean. It can also be just as dangerous to drive down the street to go to the store. In a car you take precautions. You wear a seatbelt, you obey the traffic signs and laws. These guns are just precautions to protect us while we are on the water."

"I can not believe you are comparing wearing a seatbelt to buying a gun—guns!"

It did sound kind of foolish, I admit. But she was missing the point. I tried again, "All I'm saying is that I want to protect you—us, if anything happens out there. Not that it will, but if it does, I want to be prepared. Can you try to see my side of this? I can't stand the thought of anything bad happening to you."

"How no—ble of you." She stretched the word out. But it was in her voice that I was wearing her down. I did not take any joy or pride in winning this argument. She was not quite done yet. "Has it crossed your mind that if we get into a—situation, if you pull out a gun it will just instigate and escalate the problem?"

No, I had not thought of that, but I was not about to admit it to her. I took a step forward and held out my arms. "Come on, Bree. I doubt we'll even need to take them out of their cases."

She took a reluctant step forward and entered my embrace. "That doesn't mean I have to—have to like it." There was a small sob in her voice and I felt even lower than before. I even considered calling up RJ and telling him that I did not want the guns after all.

"I'll tell you what. When we safely," I emphasized the word, "get back, and we will safely get back. I promise I'll sell the guns back to the owner of the store where I bought them. Problem solved, okay?"

It dawned on me that I had made a critical strategical error, and I waited for her to ask how much I had spent on the firearms. If it had come to that, there would have not been any telling how the night would have ended up. When she did not ask I breathed an internal sigh of relief. I changed the subject before she could think about it for too long.

"I'll tell you what else, to show you how truly sorry I am for being a jerk," I paused for dramatic effect, "I'll take you out to dinner tonight—any place you want to go."

"Why don't we just stay home and you can make me dinner instead?" She suggested.

"I'm not that sorry," I teased, and she pinched my ribs. "Ow! Hey, that hurt!"

"I'll bet you're sorry now, aren't you?"

I nodded in a rueful manner and glanced over her shoulder at the watch on my left wrist. "Alright, Brianna Hawthorne, time's running out. Offer expires soon and all that."

"And then what?"

"And then I get to choose where we eat. And I choose McDonalds." I smacked my lips.

"Not a chance."

"No, wait. You see, because this is a special occasion and all, we won't go through the drivethru, we'll actually go in and sit down. And ..." I added with the most dramatic flair I could manage, "We'll Supersize!"

Bree put the back of her hand against her forehead in a mock swoon, "Now, when everyone asks me what I see in you, I'll just tell them that I fell for you not for your brains or looks—and certainly not for your sense of humor—no, I'll tell them the reason I love you is for your excellent taste in restaurants and fine dining." Laughing, we went out to dinner, and it was not at McDonalds.

CHAPTER 4

▼

The day of our departure arrived. After bidding farewell to family and close friends, we made our way down Highway Seventeen, switched to Ninety-five South, and finally over to Twenty-six East which took us into Charleston, South Carolina. We misinterpreted our directions, which is a nice way of saying we became lost, but eventually made it over to the harbor side of the city. The irony that we were departing from the same city which Blackbeard had once laid siege to was not lost on me.

We had already signed a two week contract with a charter sailboat which was captained by a man named Caleb McSkye. He and I had discussed our trip over the phone, and he had given me concise directions to where he and his ship, *The Madora*, were docked. He had sounded a bit inebriated at the time, not exactly an auspicious beginning to our business partnership. I did not know that much about boats, other than what Caleb had told me over the phone. *The Madora* was a sixty-foot ketch with two sails. The rest of the description may as well have been in another language as far as what I could understand.

We parked on the waterfront and walked hand in hand toward where the boat was docked, moored, parked, whatever. It was a beautiful day. The sky was almost the same color as Bree's eyes, and the sun was warm in our faces. A light breeze brought the scent of the ocean to our noses and also kept the bugs away, and screeching gulls careened overhead. We approached *The Madora* and stopped. It was an impressive boat. A deckhand was mopping the deck and in general tidying things up. He noticed us, stopped what he was doing, and stood up straight. Or maybe it was that he noticed Bree first, and stopped what he was doing.

"What can I do for ya?"

I squeezed Bree's hand and answered for both of us. "We're the Thymes, Justin and Bree. We've chartered this boat for a couple of weeks." Although we were not married yet, it felt good to say our names in that way. The future Mr. and Mrs. Thyme.

"Well," he started with a grin, and I knew where this was headed. "Looks like you're here …"

"Just in time." I finished for him.

"Ya. Guess you've heard it a few thousand times before, huh?"

"At least. How soon before Captain McSkye gets here?"

He walked down the ramp to the dock. He hastily wiped his hands on the pair of faded and stained khaki shorts he was wearing and we shook hands. I was a bit confused until he said

"I'm Caleb McSkye. Nice ta meet ya." He shook Bree's hand as well, and must have seen the surprise on my face. He was not that much older than Bree and I. "I'm the captain, first mate, navigator, cook, maid, plumber, engineer, and in general Jack of all trades on board. And she's a ship, by the way, not a boat. Y'all need help with your gear?"

I was not appreciative of the fact that his eyes seldom left Bree, and he was not making eye contact with her.

"No, I think we can get it."

"Okay. Just dump it on the dock there, and we'll stow it below in a bit. Before we leave the harbor I'll give you a tour of her."

"Her?" I asked, confused. He had better not be talking about Bree, I thought.

"*The Madora*, the ship. She's a she. I mean a her. You know what I mean?"

Perhaps it was his surfer-boy look I did not like. Caleb had shoulder-length, wavy blond hair and dark blue eyes. He was deeply tanned, and the main thing holding him back from being considered handsome was that his features were feral, almost rat-like. Along with the beat up khaki shorts he was wearing, he also had on a faded blue T-shirt advertising a seafood restaurant, and some type of deck shoe. I gritted my teeth as Bree and I retraced our steps.

Safely out of range of his hearing, I asked Bree, "So, what do you think of him?"

"Caleb?" She replied in her most innocent tone of voice. I nodded. "He makes me kind of wish I had left my engagement ring in my suitcase."

"What?" I began to bluster, not realizing right off that she was just teasing me.

"Relax, Justin." She put a hand on my arm. "I didn't mean it. Why do you ask?"

"I don't like the way he was looking at you."

She smiled. "I never had you figured for the jealous type …"

I exhaled loudly in exasperation. I proceeded to pop the trunk of my car and started digging out our suitcases. We each had brought two, plus a couple of duffle bags, a backpack, and the case for my rifle. The pistol was packed away in my navy blue suitcase. We brought everything over to the dock in two trips. On the second trip Caleb noticed the rifle case.

"Is that what I think it is?"

I nodded, getting ready for—almost hoping for, an argument from him.

He shrugged instead. "Not a bad idea, can't be too careful." He eyed the pile in a critical manner, "Although that's a lotta stuff for jus' a two week trip."

We then began stowing everything below in what he said was our room, but was in fact not that much larger than our bathroom in our apartment. By 'we' I mean Bree and I did all the carrying while he walked around the deck looking over the side—for what, I do not have any idea. I think it might have just been a ploy so that he would look busy and not have to help.

When we were finished he rubbed his hands together as if wiping off dust. "Now for the tour. Fire away on any questions y'all got."

Up on the deck he asked, "Know much about ships?" We shook our heads in unison. "Okay, then. Just the basics for now. *The Madora* is a sixty-foot ketch, means she's built for speed and comfort. We have two masts, the mizzen is in the front, and the mainsail sits here in the middle. The mainsail has a self-furling boom, which is why I can handle her by myself and not need any additional crew. There's also self-steering gear which means if we wanted we could set a course and sail at night while we sleep. That's great if we're in the wide open and know the waters and if there's nobody else around. I don't usually use it though, too many bad things can happen if you ain't payin' attention." Was this supposed to relieve us? He continued his monologue. "As back up we got a big ol' diesel engine, and the fuel tanks are full. We have two radios, a commercial receiver and a radio transceiver as back up. What else?" He paused, thinking. "Oh, yeah. Once we get out on the open sea, life vests and PFD's— Personal Flotation Devices at all times. If the waters get rough and you're up on deck, we also use safety tether lines. When we're docked or at anchor the restrictions are off."

He looked at me and asked, "You like to fish?" Before I could answer in the affirmative or negative, he went on, "I know a great spot where we can hammer some Gray Snappers for dinner t'night if ya want."

Still not giving me a chance to reply, he continued, "Flares and safety gear are all back here by the wheel. I also have a cell phone, a radio phone, and walkie talkies." Caleb was thorough, I will give him that. Now if he would stop undressing Bree with his piggy little eyes I would be able to enjoy this trip.

"Am I forgetting anything?" he asked. It was a rhetorical question of course, because he had not given us a chance to get a word in edgewise so far. He did not stop now either, this was getting annoying. 'Y'all," I was beginning to hate that yokel sounding word as well. "Said you'd like to sail east toward Bermuda for a coupla days? Bo-ring." He yawned, feigning ennui. "There's not gonna be a whole lot to see, but that puts us around latitude thirty-three, same as the city of Charleston. "Y'all," I cringed. "From around here?"

I wanted to ask if we sounded like inbred rednecks, but then, that would probably have not been the best way to say that we were not from the area. So, instead we shook our heads.

"I was born and raised in SC. Not in Charleston though, just outside the city. A little place called Ladson. Don't get me wrong, the Big C. is a great city and all. A hundred thousand people living here and half of 'em are under thirty years old. Maybe that's why most people livin' in the area make over thirty-five thousand a year. I'm not one 'em, though." He laughed. "I've heard Charleston called the Cultural Capital of the South. I'm not a big history nut, but she is the second largest city in South Carolina. Hey, I'm not borin' you, am I?"

Yes. I thought. I was starting to get a headache.

"No," replied Bree. "It's very interesting. Justin was a history major in college."

"Is that so?" I was not imagining the sarcasm in his voice. "A lot of the tourists like hearing all these facts, makes 'em feel connected to the city. Plus I play a lot of Trivial Pursuit. Charleston was originally named after King Charles II, and was built on the spot where the Ashley and Cooper Rivers meet. End of history lesson."

I could have added a great deal to his generalization about the south and the city as well, but held myself in check. I did not want to encourage him to start off on another unprovoked tangent. Most major early cities were built either on or near water, however. The rivers and lakes served as a mode of travel, and a source of food as well.

For the next few minutes he scurried around like a Reese's Monkey getting the boat—ship ready to leave the harbor. Bree and I stayed out of his way as much as possible, and had already shrugged into our PFD's. I was examining what looked like a reflector on the collar when Caleb noticed my gaze and informed us, "That's a water activated strobe light. You go overboard and it starts flashing" He smiled, and I tried to gulp down the lump in my throat. Now would be a very bad time to discover I had hydrophobia.

"Alright. We're ready to roll—float—sail, whatever. Y'all can stay up front if ya want, or back here, whatever. If one of ya falls overboard, give a yell." Again the grin. When he saw we had decided to stay back in the same vicinity of the ship where he was, the boat lessons began again.

"Doppler Radar here—clear weather for now. Anemometer over here—measures wind speed. All calm for now, or at least calm enough that we'll have to use the engine to get out of the harbor. This is a Clinometer which measures roll, heel and list. The magnetic compass," he continued but I started to ignore him. Then I realized if anything happened to Caleb, Bree and I would have to fend for ourselves, so I tuned back in.

I had missed the end of his speech because he was now busy untying the ropes that kept us tied to the dock. He gave the dock a hearty kick, and as proof of Newton's law, we drifted away from it. Caleb dropped into a chair behind the wheel, mumbled something that sounded like "C'mon, baby," and turned the key. The engine coughed and started, and it was official, we were underway.

The engine burbled, making a merry sound, and the waves hissed against the bow of the boat. There was a slight flush to Bree's face, she was enjoying this, as was I. I leaned over and gave her a spontaneous kiss on the cheek, which made her smile grow even wider. We were beginning our great adventure, for better or for worse.

Speaking of that, our wedding plans had progressed well. We had narrowed down the guest list to just over a hundred and seventy-five people, and had also come up with short lists for a florist, photographer, and a church. We were still looking at reception halls. At times it seemed that for every one thing we crossed off out To-Do list, we ended up adding four or five more things that needed to be done. No complaints. No complaints at all.

Caleb began with a geography lesson. "That's Shute's Folly Island over there on the left. I mean port. Patriot's Point is a bit north of that. Fort Sumter Island is coming up on our right, starboard, and that's Sullivan's Island to our northeast. Fort Moultrie is on the point. Morris Island is to the south, and way north is Isle of Palms. Bermuda is about nine hundred miles due east, Bahamas are a little over half that distance to the southeast. Not too late to change your minds."

I was just glad that he had not expounded and gone into tedious detail about each island. We were however, moving right along, so to speak. So he did not have a lot of time to give us additional facts and figures about each little landmark.

"What do you mean it's not too late to change our minds?" Bree asked in a much more polite tone of voice than I could ever have hoped to manage.

"Well, like I said, a whole lot of nothin' between here and Bermuda. Oh, there's a bunch of ratty little unchartered islands that nobody lives on, but there's also some dangerous shouls and reefs—and they're constantly changing and moving." He paused, knowing he had our full attention. "Now, the Bahamas on the other hand, are a lot of fun. Warm water, clean white sandy beaches, insane fishing, you fish dontcha?" He had already asked that once. I did not answer then, nor did I answer now.

Bree put her head on my shoulder, "Maybe we'll change course in a few days. If that's okay?" Caleb nodded, and Bree gave him a little twist. "You're not worried about going through the Bermuda Triangle are you?"

Caleb gave a derisive snort. "Nah, only idiots get in trouble in the Triangle." My mouth went dry and I felt dizzy. "It's all bunk anyway. Although I could tell you some stories about fools that ..."

"No, that's okay." Bree interrupted him hastily and gave a hasty glance in my direction. She squeezed my hand to reassure me, and decided to change the subject. "How do reefs move?"

"Huh?" Caleb had been busy checking out a smaller powerboat going by filled with bikinis. "Reefs don't move. Shoals are like really small islands made out of sand. The tides push everything around out there, you never know what yer gonna run into. Normally I avoid the area, but hey, the money's right. Don't worry about course changes either. If we get way off course I'll just radio our new position in to the powers that be." He noticed my grim look. "You okay, man? D'you get seasick or somethin'? Why don't you go below for a while, I'll teach your wife to sail the ship."

"I'm fine." I stammered through clenched teeth, wondering where exactly I had put the M-4. And then we were into the open sea. I took another deep cleansing breath to calm myself. True, we were still in sight of land, but to the right and left, or port and starboard according to Caleb, there was only open ocean. The horizon was a flat hazy dark blue line where the sky and water met. There were a couple dozen other boats—ships, scattered like the toys of children on the water, but there were not any in our immediate vicinity.

Caleb let out a long sigh. "Oh, man, I love the ocean." Without any encouragement from us he rambled on, "The Spanish call it La Mar, which is feminine, and she can be just as beautiful or dangerous as any woman I've ever met." He glanced sideways at Bree and I again wondered just what I had gotten us into, and how long two weeks could actually be.

"Dangerous? How dangerous?" Inquired Bree, and I wanted to scream don't encourage him, we'll never get any peace and quiet. I wondered if we had packed ear plugs?

Caleb chewed on his bottom lip before answering, "People die out here. Freak storms, Rogue Waves, inexperience … But don't worry, you're safe with me."

"What's a Rogue Wave?"

"A wall of water that can be over fifty feet high, that can come from any direction without any warning at all."

I did not like the sound of that. So I asked the next question, "How often do they occur, and what do we do if we're going to get hit by one?"

"They're unpredictable. As for how often, I've been on the water since I was a kid, and I've never seen one. Sometimes they're caused by underwater earthquakes or landslides, kinda like a tsunami. If you see one comin', yell a warning and hold on!" He jerked a thumb at our life vests. "That's why you're wearing those, too."

"What about pirates?" I asked. But Caleb still wanted to talk about Rogue waves.

"A few years ago a forty footer slammed into the side of a cruise ship. It smashed windows, knocked furniture over, and scared the passengers—and crew. Pirates?" It took him a bit to acknowledge my question, and then he seemed to shrug it off. "Like Johnny Depp pirates?" He snorted. "Maybe a coupla hundred years ago, but they weren't like the ones in the movies. I've heard about modern-day pirates, and they ain't exactly what you would call nice people. But around here it's mostly just petty thieves, ya know, they go for the quick grab and go. Little stuff like fishin' gear or electronics that they can sell somewhere else. I heard down at the dock that the Somalians sometimes capture crews of freighters and then try and ransom 'em off. Is that why you brought the gun? You're afraid of pirates?"

I met his challenging gaze with one of my own. "I like to protect what's mine."

He nodded. "Fair 'nough. But again, you got no worries with Captain Caleb at the wheel!" He gazed up at the mainsail and adjusted his sunglasses. I assumed he either ran out of things to say for the moment, or he realized that we were not that interested in what he did have to say. He stopped talking. For all of about five minutes.

"We're about forty miles away from this coral reef. The Gray Snappers are spawning right now, so we should be able to catch a coupla good ones for lunch. They run about eight to ten pounds each, but fight like they weigh twice that. I heard of a record one being caught down in Florida that tipped the scales at close to twenty pounds. That is, if you wanna fish for lunch?"

I decided to try and make peace with him, or this was going to be a long trip. "Sounds like a plan." Then I made the mistake of asking, "Any advice on catching these fish? What did you call them? Gray Snappers?"

And then he was off on rambling tangent for the next half hour about bait depths, types of bait, retrieval methods and speeds, and landing the actual fish. Just when I thought I had learned more about the Gray Snapper than I had ever wanted to know before, he launched into a diatribe on methods of cooking it. These included, but were not limited to, baking, broiling, barbeque, grilled, fried, marinated, as well as in soups and stews. I grew tired just listening to him, and Bree seemed to be dozing lightly on my shoulder, her breath soft on my neck.

He stopped talking and stood up, gazing at the water. "Here we are." I looked over the side and it did not look any different than anywhere else. He began trimming the sails which consisted of lowering them and rolling them up. Both the mainsail and the mizzen had self-furling booms, so they lowered and wrapped around the support poles or booms automatically. "Gotta keep an eye on them, though," Caleb assured me. "Don't want 'em to get tangled up by accident or nothin'." Bree woke and stretched, reminding me of a cat. "Anchors away!" Caleb proclaimed, and there was a large splash off our right side.

There was a small island—if you could call it that, about a hundred yards off to one side. It looked just large enough to hold a three person tent, and not much more. One scraggy palm tree leaned precariously in the middle of the island. It reminded me of an explorer's flag proclaiming his discovery. At Caleb's encouragement, we removed our life vests.

He scrambled above and below deck and finally returned holding several heavy duty fishing poles and a rusted green tackle box.

"What's that?" Asked Bree, pointing toward the island.

"Why, that's McSkye Island. A famous reference point for the best snapper fishing north of Florida. It's also the only real shade for about fifty miles." He realized we were not swallowing it. "Okay, it's not really McSkye Island. I don't think it even has a name, but neither do a thousand other rinky-dink islands between here and Bermuda. But the fishin' is good here." He baited two hooks with what looked like something I would blow out of my nose, and handed one of the poles to me.

"You see over there where the water is a lighter green?" He pointed, "Over there?" I nodded. "That's a sweet little coral reef in there. Momma and Poppa Snapper are busy makin' baby Snappers, so cast over there and hold onto your hat, son!"

I again cringed. As I said before, he was not that much older than we were. I tripped the bail on the reel and cast where he had indicated. He clapped me hard on the shoulder, "Nice cast!"

"All this testosterone is too much for lil' ol' me," said Bree. "I think I'll go below and read for a while." It sounded like a good idea to me as well, but instead I focused on reeling in the bait at a slow pace as Caleb had suggested.

"What? Go below and miss seein' your husband catch the fish of a lifetime?" Seeing the look on her face that she was indeed not interested in watching me play Santiago, he changed his tactics. "I mean, miss this beautiful day we're having? Think of the tan you could get!"

Bree gave a demure smile, "Maybe I'll do just that. Justin, where's the sun screen?"

Ah, opportunity. "I'm not sure, you want some help finding it?"

"No," she was enjoying watching me squirm, like the booger on the end of my hook. "I can find it." She went below to change and to find everything. I continued reeling in my line. It bumped several times, but that could have been because I was on the bottom. I reeled a bit faster to raise the bait and avoid snagging my line on something.

Without warning came a tremendous jerk on the line which almost pulled the pole right out of my hands. I reeled furiously, but the line whined out of the reel as the fish took line.

"Fish on!" Caleb sang out, enjoying the show.

I lowered the pole, still reeling as fast as possible, and then lifted the rod back to a noon position. I could feel the weight of the fish, and figured I would be giving that record holder in Florida a run for his money. Dip and reel to three, raise back to twelve. I repeated this twice more, and the fish finally stopped taking out drag. I was now actually recouping some of the line the fish had taken earlier. Again, reminding me for all the world of a monkey, Caleb scampered around the deck holding a gaff in one hand, and a small wooden bat in the other.

I managed to bring the fish in close to the side of the boat. Caleb reached over with the gaff, which was a large pole with a curved hook on one end, snagged the fish, and deftly pulled it up onto the deck where it thudded almost as fast as my heart. I lifted the rod and tried to reel in the slack line, not taking my eyes off the dark brown and green pumpkin-seed shaped fish. There was a deep reddish tint on its fins. Caleb raised the bat and smacked it twice in the head. It shuddered and was still.

"Good un!" Good un? It sounded like a compliment. He extended his right hand and we shook. I noticed several thumb-sized green scales on the back of his hand. He measured it with a practiced eye. "Seven, mebbe eight, eight an' a half pounds." That was it? It had felt like twice that, five times that! I wondered if he had a scale to take an accurate weight.

Bree reappeared wearing a long, dark blue Maryland T-shirt which accentuated her bare legs. She was carrying a towel, sun screen, her I-Pod, and the latest John Grisham novel. Caleb and I watched her in silence, the fish forgotten, as she spread out her towel near the front of the boat—ship.

She removed the shirt to reveal a black string bikini. A ray of light sparkled off her barbell naval ring.

I blinked, closed my mouth, and instinctively looked at Caleb who also seemed to be under Bree's spell. I brought him back to reality, "Are we still fishing?"

He shook his head as if to clear it. "What? Oh, yeah. We need more'n this one for lunch." He placed the fish in a cooler packed with ice and re-baited my pole. I cast to one side and he to the other. We fished in contemplative silence for a bit, but I did catch him sneaking furtive looks in Bree's direction on several occasions.

I tried to hold my anger in check. Perhaps I should have felt some pride in the fact that a beautiful woman like Bree had agreed to marry me. There was a lot more to her than just her looks of course. Bree was caring, sensitive, she had a great sense of humor. She was athletic and loved all sports, enjoyed being outside, the list went on and on. She did have an exhaustive shoe collection, but if she was not perfect, she was close enough for me. Maybe that was why I did not appreciate Caleb looking at her the way he did. He saw only her external physical qualities, not the internal traits I loved her for. I also do not think his thoughts were just in admiration.

True to his word, however, the fishing was good. We would go about five to ten minutes before one of us would catch a fish. We seemed to alternate, he would catch one and then I would. After the first one we did not bother with the gaff, we would just yank them up on board, and then he would club them to death. This lasted about forty minutes before tapering off. The sun was warm and I was eyeing the water thinking how good a swim would feel. Caleb was reeling in his line nonchalantly, I think he had given up for now. I too, started to reel my line in.

There was a gentle tug, followed by a massive yank on the line unlike any of the other four fish I had caught that day. I pulled back on the pole, effectively setting the hook in the fish, which then proceeded to almost pull me overboard. I turned to shout to Caleb for help, and saw that he was staring at me incredulously. He shook his head frantically,

"No, no! Let the line snap! Break the line, Justin!"

What was he talking about? Break the line? "Caleb, I …"

He had begun digging in his tackle box. "Knife, knife, where'd I put the damn knife?"

I reeled furiously and the fish came in toward the boat. Bree had stood up and taken several tentative steps in my direction. I saw a dark flash where my line met the water. "No problem, Caleb. I've got this."

He whirled, "No, don't! It's a ..." I lifted on the pole and pulled the flopping fish up onto the deck. "It's a shark, you moron!"

Indeed it was. It was only about four feet long, but it looked a lot bigger. Maybe because it was moving around so much. It was gray on top and white on the bottom. There was a black tip on each fin, with a white band beneath that. But what held my attention was its mouth which was full of teeth. It lay there, twisting its head back and forth, snapping its jaw open and closed, almost as if it were looking for something to bite. I stood frozen, less than three feet away, and watched the shark's teeth mesmerized. I heard Bree's voice, as if from a great distance, screaming my name.

Caleb grabbed its tail and the shark twisted toward him. Its jaws closed with an audible click less than six inches from his hand. In the process of turning on him, the line did snap. He gave the shark a solid kick in the side, and it tumbled overboard with a loud splash.

"Blacktip Reef Shark," he gasped, panting. "You okay?"I nodded, all thoughts of going for a swim fading fast. "They're pretty common, although I've never seen one out here."

Bree was at my side, and I could smell the sun screen she wore. Something fruity.

Caleb flashed his obnoxious grin. "We weren't fishin' for sharks. I tried to warn you, dude." He gave Bree a long admiring look. "He doesn't listen too well, does he?" Not waiting for an answer, he went on, "Well, fishing's done for the day, anyhow. Now I'll show ya my famous gutting method for cleaning fish." In light of all that had happened already, I could hardly contain my excitement.

CHAPTER 5

▼

Caleb could cook, I will give him that. He made some type of marinade for the fish that used alcohol as the main ingredient. There was also a light salad and a bottle of white Zinfandel as well. I never really understood why it was referred to as white zin when it was actually a blush wine. Japhet had been a big wine connoisseur, and had explained it all to me. The wine is kept pale by removing the skins after the grapes have been pressed. White zin is usually a sweet wine, that is considered off-dry. It is actually a rose wine, and is often pinkish in color.

Fortunately, Caleb had cleaned the fish while I watched. It was a messy affair, and he kept up a running monologue the entire time. Bree had gone below to change into a less revealing outfit, or maybe I should say less distracting outfit. I think she had finally noticed his blatant stares. After he had cleaned and filleted the fish, he unceremoniously dumped all of the entrails, heads, and fins over the side and into the water. Then he had brought up a small grill, made the marinade, and begun dinner. He had talked the entire time, and I wondered if he was one of those people who also talked in their sleep. I would not have doubted it for a moment.

Anything left over from dinner was also dumped over the side. I noticed Bree's look of consternation, but it was all bio-degradable. I know that does not excuse his actions, but he was the captain, and he had dumped the refuse without a moments hesitation. Maybe it was common practice out here on the water. Perhaps it would be best if I tried to get on his good side or in his good graces, and stay there.

The more Caleb drank, the louder he became. He easily drank at least half the bottle of wine by himself. As the sun began to set he started telling some off color jokes. Bree actually winced at a couple of them before excusing herself.

"I think I'll go below," she looked at me. "It's been a long day."

To be polite, I stayed up on deck a while longer. The wind and the waves were pleasant background noise as Caleb and I watched the sun set. He got up, stretched, and then moved around the deck turning on several electric lights. From somewhere he procured a six-pack of long neck Coronas, and he amiably handed one to me. We touched bottles and then he was running off at the mouth again.

"Not bad for a first day, 'cept for the shark. One down, thirteen to go. Lucky thirteen." He burped and scratched his stomach. "That was a pretty good meal, if I say so myself."

"Yes, it was. Thanks."

He waved my appreciation away as if shooing flies. "No worries, man. Y'all are payin' me well to do what I love most in the world." He looked up into the rigging where the wind was making a lonely sighing sound. "It don't get much better'n this." He studied his beer bottle for a long moment.

"Look, Caleb, I'm—sorry about the shark thing today."

He frowned. "Ah, no big deal. No blood, no foul. There's a lot nastier things you could've pulled on board. I've seen sharks that will chase after you on the deck, not like that little one you pulled on board."

"He didn't look so small from where I was standing." I took a pull from my bottle.

Caleb laughed, "Ya, he was a good un. A keeper if we were trophy fishin'. Have it stuffed and mounted an' put on the wall in your office to impress your clients."

"I don't have an office. I'm a teacher." And just like that I knew when we returned I would not be working for Japhet. That meant I had some unpleasantness to deal with, but it would be a couple of weeks away, and Bree and I could find some easy way to tell him.

My admonition seemed to surprise him. "A teacher! Whaddya teach?"

I was tempted to say English, but I did not think he would get it. "High school History, or I will be in the fall, anyway."

"If ya don't mind me askin'," He waved a hand around, encompassing the ship. "How's a teacher pay for all of this?"

I hesitated, not sure if I wanted to share a lot—or any, personal information with Caleb. But seeing as how we were now both on our third beers, I plowed on.

"My dad gave me some money when I graduated college. This is kind of a pre-honeymoon trip for Bree and I."

He nodded. "Ya, I figured about as much." He finished his Corona and launched the bottle over the side and into the water. "But if I was you, I wouldn't be up here talkin' with me right now." He nodded toward the hatch leading below.

I finished my third bottle and stood up, reaching for the mast for support. I admit it, I was a little shaky in the knees. My eyes met Caleb's, and I hesitated a moment before tossing my bottle over the side as well. "Thanks for dinner and the beer. Good night, Captain."

The compliment seemed to please him. As I stared down the hatch to go below, he said, "Maybe tomorrow we'll row over to an island. Bree can sun herself on the beach in privacy while you and I fire off a few rounds in the jungle."

"Sounds good." And it did. I had only fired the M-4 that one time, at RJ's indoor range. A little extra practice would not hurt. It would be fun to explore too. Kind of a Huck Finn, *Lord of the Flies* thing. Only we would be armed. I was still mulling it over when I tapped on the door going into our room.

"Bree? It's me." I was not sure if I liked the idea of being around Caleb when he had a weapon, however. Too many convenient accidents were possible. Maybe I was just being paranoid. I opened the door and went into our room. She had been unpacking, or was still in the process of unpacking. I playfully slapped her on the bottom.

"Hey!" She turned and then wrinkled her nose. "Have you been drinking?"

"Guilty, as charged." I gave her my most lecherous grin, growled, and then picked her up and tossed her on the bed. I pounced on her, still growling, and started kissing her neck and tickling her.

"Justin!" She said between bouts of laughter, "Stop!" She hit me in the head with the pillow. One last kiss and I collapsed beside her to catch my breath. Both of us were smiling like fools.

Bree braced herself up on one elbow and looked at me. "I'm marrying a complete fool."

"Is he bigger than me?" She rolled her eyes and I continued, "So what do you think of our captain?"

"Haven't we been through this once already?"

"Yeah, but those were first impressions." I paused, trying to figure out how to put my thoughts into coherent words. How well could you truly know someone after less than a day? "I'm talking about second and third impressions, now."

Bree shrugged. "He seems harmless. A lot of bluster and talk, typical of most men I know."

"Oh really?" I asked. I reached over and turned off the light, and then proceeded to show her that I for one, was not all bluster and talk.

Day two on the briny seas turned out to be a carbon copy in regards to the weather as the day before. Bree and I got cleaned up, dressed, and then went up on deck to where Caleb had prepared some type of fruit cup and smoothie for breakfast. We were still anchored by the reef where we had caught the previous day's lunch. The sky was a dark, clear blue, and cloudless.

"How'd you guys sleep last night?" He asked grinning. I realized with a sick feeling in my stomach that he had almost certainly heard us.

"Fine," I replied in a cautious tone of voice. "How about you, Caleb?"

"Oh," he stretched in an exaggerated manner. "I slept well. I like sleeping up here on the deck in the open air." I breathed a silent sigh of relief, and then he added, "It's quieter." Bree blushed and I contemplated pushing him over the side.

He glanced down at his wristwatch. "We'll get underway here in a few minutes. I know of a larger island a couple hours east of here where we can have some lunch and do some exploring." He saw Bree and I exchange nervous glances. "Oh, it's not dangerous or anything. Besides," he added, "You'll probably want to get some target practice in with your guns." Then in a facetious tone he added, "You don't want your sharpshooter skills to get rusty in case we run into some pirates or something."

We put on our life vests—PFDs. Caleb raised the sails, and we were on our way again. As a nice change, the morning passed in relative silence and without event. I sat up near the bow watching the waves and contemplating the possibility that my mother had once been in this very same area twenty years ago. The real purpose of this trip was never far in my thoughts. Was it possible that Erich Craigie was still alive? Was there any chance that I might find him in all this vast nothingness? A needle in a stack of needles indeed.

My reverie was interrupted by Caleb calling Bree back in order to teach her to sail the boat—ship. Would I ever get that right? It was a clever ruse to get her in close proximity to where he was standing. She was wearing a forest green one piece today, with a pair of khaki cargo shorts as well. Caleb was either wearing the same clothes as the day before, or an outfit very similar to it. I concentrated on the waves.

"Justin, come on back. It's easy!" She called moments later.

I stood up, feeling both tired and old for some reason, and made my way back to where they were manning the wheel.

"Easy as drivin' a car," Caleb crowed, and it was. Even better, for once he was able to keep his mouth shut for an extended period of time. "Jus' keep her on this headin' boss," he directed. Caleb leaned back, pulled his hat over his eyes, and put his feet up on the rail.

Bree cast a nervous glance in his direction. "You're not really going to go to sleep, are you?"

Mock snoring from Caleb. I did not care as long as he remained quiet for a change. We sailed on in relative silence. After about ten minutes, I started to relax. I could handle this. I call it a relative silence because there were constant noises. The wind and the waves were a steady whisper, and water slapped against the hull. There was also the creak of the ship itself. Where the bow split the waves there was a constant splashing gurgle of water. It was very relaxing.

An indefinite time later, a smudge appeared on the horizon. That is the only way I can think to describe what I saw. It looked like someone had smeared a pencil mark where the water met the sky. I squinted, and was reaching for the binoculars Caleb kept handy to check out bikinis when Bree asked, "Is that a boat?"

This roused our fearless leader who sat up yawning and rubbing his eyes. He made a big show out of stretching, stood up, and took the binoculars from my hand to look for himself.

"Nope. No boat. That's the island we want." He looked at me. "Nice job ... captain."

Again the sarcasm. I let it go, again. I wondered if by letting him get away with all of this foolishness if I was just encouraging him to walk all over me. I considered standing up for myself and letting him know where the lines were drawn and that he had best not cross them. Although the facetiousness was a petty thing, I decided to wait until later to address the problem. With Caleb, you could always count on there being a later or a next time.

The smudge grew more distinct as we drew closer. I was able to discern a mass of trees, then a sandy beach, and at last, individual trees and features. It was a sizable island, at least in comparison to what we had seen so far. I could see both ends, but not across the width. There was also some elevation to it. We dropped anchor and furled the sails. Caleb walked over to the edge of the ship and peered down into the water. I looked overboard as well. The water was clear and I could see the bottom about fifteen feet away.

"Anyone for a swim?" He inquired. Bree and I looked at each other and then watched in amazement as Caleb removed his shirt and dove overboard with a loud splash.

"Aren't you worried about sharks?" Asked Bree.

His reply was nonchalant, "Nah. If I was worried about all of the things in the ocean that could kill me, I would never leave land." He was treading water about a dozen feet away and looking up at us. "Y'all gonna join me, or what?" He glanced over his shoulder, "What was that?"

I started to stand up as Caleb sank beneath the waves without warning. He resurfaced and started yelling, "Help! Shark!" My eyes darted around frantically for something to help him. He vanished beneath the waves again. I reached for a life preserver hooked to the side of the boat. It would not do much good, but it was something. Where was the gaff we had used?

"Caleb!" Screamed Bree. I tossed the preserver in his direction and then started to climb over the rail. To do what, I do not have any idea. Caleb resurfaced. He was laughing.

"Oh, man, you should've seen your faces!" He looked to where I had stopped in mid-climb. "What were you gonna do, jump in and fight off a shark bare handed?"

"Actually I was thinking of strangling you." He swam over to the boat, and I reached out a hand and helped pull him back on board. "That wasn't funny, Caleb." I looked over at Bree, she was really shaken up. Her face was red, and there was a hitch as she breathed. That angered me even more.

"Aw, c'mon, man. You'd be surprised how many people have been swimming in the ocean and there was a shark less then ten feet away from them. Happens olla time. Ignorance is bliss, an' all that malarkey."

Ignorance, maybe. But not flat out stupidity. He toweled off quickly and began maneuvering the ten-foot dingy over the side. There was a small outboard motor attached to it, and he spent an additional fifteen minutes or so getting it started.

"You gonna go and get your rifle, or stand there all day?" He asked, glancing up at me. I was tempted to tell him that he did not want to be around me if I had a loaded weapon in my hands. Instead, I looked at the smaller boat and asked, "That thing going to hold all three of us?"

"Course," was his one word reply. He managed to make it sound like I was a fool for even asking. I was still unsure about it, but then Bree solved the problem for us.

"You boys go on ahead. I'm going to stay here and work on my tan and finish my book."

I shrugged and went below to get the M-4 and some ammunition. I handed it down to Caleb who was already in the smaller craft, and then climbed in myself.

"She going to be okay," I asked him, nodding in Bree's direction, "All by herself?"

"Yeah, she'll be fine. You're not still worried about pirates are ya?" He saw that I was. "Look, I'm telling you, there are no pirates around here. You're thinkin' Somalia, or places like that. We're perfectly safe." He patted the gun case, as if it were an obedient dog. "Besides, we have this." He yanked on the engine cord and it sputtered to life in a cloud of smoke. He fiddled and faddled with a couple protruding parts and the sound smoothed out.

"Hey," he asked. "Why can't little kids go to the pirate movie?"

Now what was he talking about? Maybe it was a joke. "Why?"

"Cause it's rated arrrr." He laughed. I had to admit, that was a good one. "Okay, okay, where do pirates go for vacation?" He did not wait for me to ask where, but in typical Caleb fashion just plowed on, "Arrrr-ruba." Not as funny. "What did one pirate ask the other pirate?" I did not know, but I had an idea it probably had something to do with the word 'argh.' "Arghh you talkin' to me?"

I did not crack a smile, so maybe he got the point. We motored toward the beach. I cast an anxious look over my shoulder to where Bree now lay stretched out on the deck, offering her body to the sun. It was something of a relief when I realized that she was not that far away. In fact, she was in shouting distance. I tested this theory, "I miss you, baby!"

She hollered right back, "If you missed me, you wouldn't have left me here alone!"

"Turn around," I directed Caleb. He laughed, but did not turn around. Moments later he pulled the engine out of the water and we coasted into shore, beaching gently in the sand. We exited the boat and walked over the pristine white sand to where the trees offered some shade. I opened the case and Caleb let out a low whistle of appreciation at the sight of the gun.

"An M-4, you don't believe in messin' around, do ya?"

It still had an oily sheen and I could smell the lubricant. The rifle was solid in my hands, and I could feel the power in it, waiting to be awakened. I took a loaded clip with twenty rounds in it and slammed it home. Checking to make sure the safety was on, I pulled back the bolt, which put a round into the chamber. It was now loaded and ready to be fired. Our eyes met, and he nodded for me to go first.

Even though we were outside, it seemed much louder than when I was at the firing range. Also, neither one of us was wearing ear protection, although Caleb had plugged his ears with his fingers. I fired six rounds into a dangerous looking palm tree about twenty feet away. The four that hit made holes the size of my fist in the trunk. The other two shots whined away into the distance. I was very careful not to shoot in the direction of Bree and the boat. In the silence that followed, some gulls screamed indignantly at the interruption of silence. I squeezed off four more rounds at a group of coconuts hanging in the tree. I thought I had missed, but was surprised when several fell to the ground. I clicked the safety to on and handed the rifle to Caleb.

"I don't think you hit any," was all he said. He then made a big show of examining the gun and putting it on its side and then sighting down the barrel. Seemingly satisfied, he extended the stock to the next setting back, and then placed it firmly against his shoulder. He squeezed off three quick shots in succession. Two of the coconuts on the ground exploded in a milky spray, and the third spun off into the jungle. He grinned. This was obviously someone who knew their way around guns.

"It shoots a bit low, but it's a sweet gun." He fired off another three rounds and a half dozen coconuts fell out of a tree. "We'll bring back some coconuts for Bree." He switched on the safety and handed the rifle back to me. There were four shots left. He nodded toward the coconuts on the ground, "Sight in on one and see if you can hit it. Pretend it's someone's head." I did not want to tell him whose head I was imagining as I squeezed the trigger once. I missed.

"I was told head shots aren't accurate."

"Yeah, but even with a rifle like that, a body shot is not always going to stop a man. Dontcha watch the movies?" Indeed I did. But how much was fact and how much was sensationalism? I squeezed off the second and third shot and sand in front of the targets sprayed up into the air. One more. It had been so much easier in the cool indoor range with RJ. I was rewarded on the last shot with the coconut exploding. Caleb clapped me hard on the shoulder with his hand. I found myself wondering if a man's head would explode like that as well.

I clicked the safety and ejected the now empty clip. Then I checked the rifle to make sure I had not counted wrong and that there still was not a round in the chamber. It was empty.

"Make sure you wipe that down well with oil when we get back. The salt air will really take its toll on a nice little rifle like that."

I slung the M-4 over my shoulder, and we each grabbed a couple of coconuts. We carried them back to the motorboat. I glanced out toward where Bree was still laying on the deck. She was safe. I climbed into the boat, then Caleb gave us a push out into the shallows before climbing in as well. The engine started on the first try, and we made our way back in silence to *The Madora* and Bree. I noticed a dark line of clouds on the distant horizon to the west.

"Storm comin', I think," stated Captain Obvious. I did not have a lot of experience on the water, but even I could tell that. I wondered how bad it would be, or if it would miss us.

The wind had picked up a bit, and Bree had changed into wind pants and a long sleeved shirt by the time we got back. She was also looking at the line of storm clouds to the west. Caleb was all business, moving efficiently around the ship, stowing gear and double checking all the latches and windows.

"What can I do to help?" I asked, wanting to do something—anything.

He looked up from the coil of rope that he was winding around his forearm, and then back at the clouds. "You want to help?" He repeated, and I nodded. "Put on your PFD and go below. Find something to hold onto in case we roll."

"Roll!" I did not like the sound of that. Roll implied upside down and a watery death.

"Yeah, roll." With his pointer finger he drew a large slow circle in the air. "If the waves get real bad and we get caught wrong, we'll roll over. But don't worry," he finished his knot. "The ballast should pop us back upright again."

Should? Don't worry? I swallowed a lump in my throat. "Are we staying here? Should we radio for help? What are we going to do?" Even I could hear the panic rising in my voice.

"We," he put emphasis on the word. "Are going to try and outrun this thing, depending on how bad it gets. I," again he paused, "Will use the radio if it's needed. You," another pause, are going below to keep your pretty fiancee calm. I'll let you know if I need you."

"I thought the weather report called for clear weather this week?"

Caleb took several menacing steps in my direction. Not liking to be crowded, I retreated a couple of steps. "Welcome to the Bermuda Triangle, Justin." Then he laughed without humor. "And when have you ever known a weatherman to accurately predict the weather? Now go below. Please." He added, almost as an afterthought, "I'll have enough to worry about up here without you running around in a near panic. We're gonna be fine."

Who was I to argue? Not wanting to bother him further, I went below and helped Bree into her PFD. Her eyes were wide, and I tried to act calm, for her sake. At least that was what I told myself. We sat on our bed, holding hands tightly. I am not sure how long we sat there, but the hand that Bree was squeezing was beginning to go numb.

Caleb had turned on the engines and we could feel the movement of the ship. The air felt heavy, almost oppressive. Nervous, I licked my dry lips and listened to myself breathe. The hatch opened without warning and Bree gasped in surprise, jumping a little.

"Justin? I'm gonna need you up here, I think."

The pressure in my hand increased to what I thought may be the breaking point. I turned and gave her a fierce kiss. "Don't worry about me," I said with as much bravado as I could muster, "I'll be back soon."

"Justin …" I kissed her again.

"Let's go, man. I need your help now."

Up on the deck he handed me what looked like a short length of rope. "It's a tether line. If you go overboard it will keep you hooked to the boat." One end hooked to my PFD, the other attached to the life line that went around the deck, just below the bottom rail. He clipped the tether line to my PFD and looked hard at me. "If you go over, you're on your own. I'll be too busy with the ship. If I go over …" He did not finish, nor did he need to.

The waves had gotten much larger, but I did not think we had to worry about them washing over the deck. The sky was a wet slate color, and the wind had picked up as well. Caleb had lowered the sails and tied them off.

"What do you want me to do?"

"First, don't get washed or thrown overboard. Second, I want you to watch for large waves—Rogue Waves. With the wind picking up, they can come from any direction at any time. Keep an eye peeled for anything that comes loose on the deck as well. This is getting worse, and we're not gonna outrun it. That curtain behind us?" He nodded back over his shoulder. It did indeed look like a curtain connecting the sky and the waves. "That's rain. I hope you don't mind gettin' a little wet."

Little was not the correct adjective. It started out as a few drops and I was thinking it was not so bad, when somebody turned the faucet on full. It was literally like standing in a shower with your clothes on.

"Here we go!" Shouted Caleb. He handed me a yellow raincoat which went on over my already soaked T-shirt and shorts which I had on from earlier. The rain picked up, if that was possible, and the size of the waves increased. *The Madora* rode through them without a problem. This was not so bad. Maybe Caleb had been wrong about the severity of the storm.

Then the thunder and lightening arrived, and I realized I had new things to learn about storms at sea. The wind and rain increased as well, and visibility decreased to about fifty feet. Drops of water stung my face from all directions, and the wind tugged at my clothes in a hungry manner. I slid and slipped back to where Caleb was battling the wheel, pulling my tether after me.

With water streaming down his face like angel tears, he shouted to be heard above the roar of the storm, "We're gonna try and get on the other side of one of the islands where the water's deeper. We'll be sheltered from the worst of the wind, and the waves won't be so bad."

So that was why we had not stayed where we were earlier. The waves increased in size in shallow water, and we had only been in about a dozen feet. We were caught broadside by a wave and there was a crash from below. I heard a faint scream from Bree, and made for the hatch.

Caleb grabbed at me. "If you open that hatch and a wave catches us wrong, it'll flood below and sink us. I, oh—crap."

I looked up. At first my mind refused to accept what I was seeing. What looked like a wall of water, seeming to stretch to the sky, was roaring right at us. Right at me, it seemed.

"Hold on!" Then there was water up my nose, and in my eyes, ears and mouth. I am still not sure if the wave just broke over us, or if we were completely submerged. It was as bad as a moment as I have ever been in. We popped back out the other side, and the foamy water was still knee deep where I was standing. I saw Caleb was still at the wheel, spitting out water. As the wave receded, I was swept off my feet and carried with it toward the bow of the ship. At the last minute I was able to grab a rail which kept me from going overboard. As it was, my legs and thighs were hanging out over the water. I tried to yell but had a mouthful of water.

Straining, I kicked and pulled myself back on board, and then half crawled, half slithered back to where Caleb was still battling the wheel.

"Is this the most fun you've had in a while, or what?"

"Or what," I answered, and he laughed.

A bolt of lightening lit up the sky and I felt like target practice for the God I was starting to believe in. I was oddly reminded of the day I had sighted in my M-4 at the target range. Was some higher power sighting in on me right now? I shook my head to clear it, wondering if I had bumped it when I fell earlier.

"This ain't so bad," the great talker was at it again. I gave him a quizzical look. "This is only a four, mebbe a five on the Beaufort Scale." He saw my confused look. "It measures storm severity and intensity. The higher the number, the worse the storm. I've been in some eights before, but I wouldn't wanna do it again." Was he bragging, or trying to reassure me? I decided the former was more his style.

Another large shape loomed up in front of us. I almost panicked before realizing it was another island. Caleb skillfully guided us around to the back side of it where there was a somewhat sheltered bay. He dropped both anchors, but left the engines running. The weather was still quite intense, but not anything like it had been in the open water.

"Look," he nodded off to the right. In the distance, on the other side of the bay was another ship. I could see the masts, but the sails were down. I could not see much else. "I guess we weren't the only ones that got caught out in this mess."

"Should we radio them to see if they're okay or not?"

He shrugged. "Let's wait and see if the storm calms down a bit. If they were in any trouble they would probably have radioed us or sent an SOS. Besides," he paused, thinking about the best way to word his next statement. "I'm not too big on approaching ships unannounced. You're not the only one out here packed for bear, ya know."

Caleb gazed up into the sky and opened his mouth to allow some rain water to wash down his throat. I am not sure he could be thirsty after the drenching we were taking and had taken.

"You can go back below, now. I think we're going to be okay. Keep your ears open, though. If it picks back up, and I need you, I'll give a yell."

I turned toward the hatch after casting a wary eye at the waves. His voice calling my name stopped me. "Justin?" I turned back toward him, and he was nodding in approval, "You did good today, real good."

Feeling as if I had just passed a major test, and in his eyes, perhaps I had, I went below to make sure that Bree was okay.

CHAPTER 6

▼

The next morning a few thin clouds chased each other across a dark blue sky. It was warm enough that we were comfortable in shorts and t-shirts. Except for some floating debris, it was almost as if the storm had never happened at all. It was as if it had all been a bad dream. Some luggage and other gear had fallen out of the storage cabinets below, but that had been quickly and efficiently picked up. Caleb also made a complete meticulous inspection of the ship. It took over an hour before he pronounced us good to go.

Bree and I had also gone up on deck to see if we could contribute anything. We had pinned some wet clothes to the rail, and the morning wind was drying them out. All three of us were a bit bleary eyed from lack of sleep. I yawned and stretched. The morning sun was warm and felt good. My shoulder was a bit tight, and I assumed that I had pulled a muscle in it when the wave had almost washed me overboard. Almost. Caleb's words about being on my own if that had happened caused a shiver to run down my spine.

Speaking of our fearless leader, and I felt a twinge of guilt. He had brought us through the storm safe. Caleb raised a pair of binoculars to his eyes and turned toward the other ship. He raised a hand and waved. "I see you, and you see me." He passed the binoculars to me and explained, "They're looking at us, too." I looked and was dizzy for a moment until I found the other ship. It was difficult to focus because of the bobbing waves, but there was definitely someone standing on the deck of the smaller sailboat. A ray of sun glinted of the binoculars in the other man's hand.

"Well, let's go say howdy-do." Caleb started the engine, let it run for a long moment, and then turned the *Madora* in the direction of the other ship. He was uncharacteristically quiet this morning. As usual, that did not last long. "Hey, Bree, what say you go down into the galley and make us some coffee?"

Now, while Bree is not exactly an ardent feminist, she is politically correct. And that request definitely smacked of sexism. I waited for her to tell Caleb to brew it himself, or for her to throw him overboard, but neither happened. Imagine my surprise when she turned and went meekly below. I watched the entire scene with my mouth open.

"If I had suggested that, you'd be picking me up off the deck right now."

Caleb chuckled, but then turned serious. "I actually didn't want her on deck when we make contact with that other ship. And I would appreciate it if you kept an eye on them while I steer."

It was not like him to be so cautious. It made me worry to see him like this. "Are you expecting some trouble with them? What's the big deal?"

He hesitated. "No. Not really. But you can never be too sure or too careful. A lot of people out here just want to be left alone. Then there's drug runners, smugglers, insurance scams. Y'know, people who don't like others nosin' around in their bidness. Just keep an eye on 'em, willya?"

I nodded and again raised the binoculars to my eyes. We were closer and I was able to determine that the storm had not done any exterior damage to the other ship. There was not anyone in sight on the deck. I voiced my discovery, and added, "I wonder where he went?"

"Down below to hide anything he doesn't want us to see, and to probably get his own gun."

"Own gun?" Do you want me to go get the M-4?"

He snorted. "And I thought you didn't watch a lot of movies? No, if he has a gun, it'll be a pistol, and it will be tucked into his waistband." Caleb lifted the edge of his shirt to show me the pistol he had tucked in there.

The surprises never ended around here. He grinned at me. "I told you, you can never be too careful out here."

For once Caleb was wrong. Unfortunately. As we drew closer the other man reappeared on deck with his own assault rifle strapped around his neck. This did not look good.

"Oh, crap." The last time he had said those two words together we had almost been swamped and sunk. Caleb cut the engine and turned the *Madora* broadside to the other ship. This may have been a tactical error on his part because we now presented a much broader target. We were about thirty feet away, and it was not likely that the other guy would miss from such a short range, unless he was an even worse shot than me. This I doubted just by observing the way he held the weapon. The man held the rifle in a ready position. It was pointed down, but all he needed to do was lift it eighteen inches and it would be pointed right at us. He could pull off this maneuver in less than two seconds.

"Ahoy!" Shouted Caleb through cupped hands to amplify his voice. The stress of the moment for some strange reason made me want to shout Chips! I did not think this was a good idea, despite how funny it would sound. I was barely able to contain my panicked laughter.

"What do you want? Are you alone?" Came the response. His hands stayed on the rifle.

"We just wanted to make sure you got through the storm okay. There's three of us on board. I'm Caleb McSkye," he nodded in my direction. "That's Justin, uh, Time. And his fiancee is below. Are you hoofin' it alone out here?" I thought he was being a bit nosey and that maybe we would be better off just taking our leave while the taking was good.

The other sailor seemed to relax a bit at the mention of Bree. But not by much.

"Yeah, we made it through the storm just fine. I see you did also. And my fiancee is below deck as well." Silence. We were at a stalemate. I was about to suggest that we leave when Caleb whispered just loud enough for me to hear,

"Yeah, right. We'll show you ours if you show us yours, first." To me he said out of the corner of his mouth, "I don't like this. Maybe we had better just get goin'. Don't make any sudden moves until we're well away. That's an M-16 he's holding."

"What're you guys whispering about?" He started to raise the gun when Bree came up on the deck holding three steaming mugs of coffee. Time seemed to stop. I looked from Bree to the M-16, and then to Caleb and back to the M-16 again.

"That your fiancee?" He seemed confused. Unsure now. My witty response normally would have been 'no, she's my brother,' but I did not think that would be wise in this case. So I nodded and he lowered the rifle so that it was now perpendicular to his side. "I'm Jaffe O'Neill." He paused and then called to his deck, "Hey Mar, c'mon up. It's okay."

Now please do not get me wrong here, I am dedicated and loyal to Bree. I have never cheated on her, nor have I had any inclination to do so. I would never do anything to hurt her either. But the woman who came up onto the deck of the neighboring ship was drop dead beautiful. She could have been a model, that is how attractive she was. I know that sounds piggish and sexist and typical male chauvinist scum talk, but it was the truth.

Mar had long, dark hair. She was tall and slender, and built like a runner. Her muscle tone was smooth and flowed from one muscle group to the next, and she was in very good shape. She had a dark, even tan, and very clear cut facial features. From this distance it looked like her eyes were the same color as the sky. I noticed we had drifted closer to their ship as we had been talking. Mar was wearing a loose T-shirt and shorts, and strings of her bathing suit peeked out here and there.

"This is my fiancee, Marissa." I again looked at Jaffe. He was built like a wrestler, hard knotty bunches of muscles in his arms, legs, and neck. He had a severe crewcut which kept his light brown hair in check. His eyes were dark, and he wore a white tank top and multi-colored Bermuda shorts that hung below his knees. There was a small crescent moon shaped scar on his right shoulder. We were getting close, now. "C'mon over," and then he added, "But don't try anything foolish." We did not need to be told twice.

Caleb tossed him a rope and then it was a simple process to pull us over. "Drop the bumpers," he directed, and then in an annoyed tone of voice at my confusion, "The rubber pill-shaped things. They'll keep the hulls from scrapin' each other."

Jaffe seemed reluctant to put away the M-16 now that we were so close. As Caleb went about securing our two ships together, Jaffe asked, "Anything you want to tell me now?"

I paused for a moment. This was probably not the time for wit, so I tried honesty instead and hoped for the best. "I have an M-4 and a Glock pistol down below in our gear."

He chortled in amusement. "No, I meant anything illegal. You know, drugs, or anything like that?" I wondered what else besides drugs people would smuggle. People? Weapons?

"If we did, would we tell you? Or why would you even believe us in the first case?"

He nodded. "Good point. But there needs to be some trust between our two ships." As a show of good faith he unslung the M-16 and placed it inside a hatch. He held up his right hand, "I solemnly swear Mar and I are not involved in anything illegal. At this time."

So he had a sense of humor. Feeling foolish I repeated his words and actions. Bree and Marissa were already chatting away like two old friends. Caleb had finished his elaborate song and dance between the two ships, and after taking a good eyeful of the women, walked over to the two of us. Typical of Caleb, he broke into our conversation,

"Where y'all headin'?" Subtlety was not his forte.

Jaffe, seeming more relaxed now, answered without hesitation, "There's not a whole lot out here to see. We were going to try for Bermuda, but I'm thinking of swinging south instead and hitting the Bahamas, maybe the Keys, Bimini. We've got plenty of supplies to last us."

"Bermuda is only about a day away, Nassau is at least a day and a half, and that's if there ain't any more storms."

"We'll be fine," Jaffe said with conviction, and I believed him. The girls came over.

"Mar and I were thinking of steak for lunch, how does that sound to you guys?"

I looked at Jaffe and Caleb, they nodded. "Sounds good to us."

"Great. When are you going to start cooking it?"

I clapped my hand to my forehead, "I've been set up!" I said amidst the laughter

It took a while to set up the grill and get everything going. Some of the gear we had stowed away before the storm had shifted and it was all tangled together in the storage compartments. While Jaffe and I were firing up the grill and marinating the steak, Caleb had convinced the two girls to join him for a swim. How typical.

Jaffe eyed him warily, "What's your captain's story, anyway?"

I shrugged. "I've only known him a couple of days." I placed a steak on the grill and it sizzled, sending up a cloud of fragrant smoke. Had it really only been a couple of days? It seemed like I had been on the *Madora* with Caleb a lot longer than that.

"I don't know," Jaffe mused. "Caleb makes me ... uneasy, I guess is the word."

"Yeah," I agreed. "Me too. But I think—I'm pretty sure, anyway, that he's harmless."

"To us." He nodded toward the swimmers, "But what about them?"

I did not answer. Instead I concentrated on flipping the steaks. Flames shot up.

"Hey," Jaffe called to the trio in the water. "Anyone want a beer?"

Caleb immediately began swimming back to the ship. Those were magic words to him. If there was anything he liked better than bikinis it was beer. After a moment's hesitation, the girls followed. I guess he was thirsty because it did not take him very long to get back and climb on board. He reached greedily for the cold bottle Jaffe was holding. After a long swallow, he smacked his lips in appreciation and looked toward where the girls were still swimming toward the ship.

"Those certainly are a couple of fine lookin' women you guys have there."

Jaffe chose a tactful remark as I focused my attention on the steaks, "Yes. We certainly are lucky men. What about you, Caleb? Do you have a first mate for your ship?"

He took another long pull on his bottle and cackled, "That's a good one. First mate. Oh, man, I'll hafta remember that one. Well, I'll tell ya. There is a Mrs. McSkye and two boys back home in good ol' S.C."

I felt sorry for them, and then pointed out the obvious, "But no ring," I said, nodding toward his bare left hand. I took my eyes of the girls for a moment to make eye contact with him. They were only a few feet from the ship now anyway.

"Course not," responded Caleb. "My girlfriends," He emphasized the pluralness of the word and winked lecherously, "Would not approve of a wedding band around my neck—I mean finger." He laughed again. "I hope there's more beer in that cooler?"

"Help yourself." But Caleb was already doing just that. He dug around in the ice and among the bottles trying to find a specific one. The steaks were okay for the time being, so Jaffe and I grabbed a couple of towels and brought them back to the girls. They were just emerging from the water, and were laughing about something.

"Thank you," was Marissa's response when I reached down and gave her a hand. She emerged from the water sleek and shining. As I pulled Bree out I took her in my arms surprising her by giving her a long kiss. Her hair was dark from the water.

"I thought you were cooking dinner?" She inquired.

"If it burns, we'll order take out," she laughed, remembering. I looked back to where Caleb was now on his third or maybe fourth beer. He was flipping the steaks in an expert manner that surprised me.

"It's taken care of. Are you going to change into something dry or parade around in a wet bathing suit for the rest of the day?

She gave me a coquettish smile, "The sun will dry me off soon enough."

"Slop's on!" Called Caleb. Slop? I shook my head at the wondering looks on Marissa and Jaffe's faces. Caleb took some getting used to. After two days I still was not used to him, if in fact I ever *would* get used to him. Somehow, I doubted it. Two days down, almost three, I reminded myself.

Another little voice in the back of my head painfully reminded me that there were still at least eleven more to go. I pushed the little voice away. It was even more annoying than Caleb. If that were possible.

The five of us sat cross-legged on the deck and ate lunch. Caleb had also taken some vegetables from the ship's stores and steamed them. There was also plenty of alcohol. I found myself wondering where he kept it all, and how much he had brought along. The answer to the second seemed to be plenty. We spent the afternoon drinking and socializing.

As the sun grew hotter, we all went our separate ways for a nap. Bree's hair was still damp, and held a faint smell of the ocean when she snuggled against me. Before dozing off, she murmured, "I like Mar and Jaffe. They're nice."

I was inclined to agree, and mumbled, "Mm-hm," as I was falling asleep as well. Moments later, I was.

I awoke with a start, feeling achy, sluggish, and sore from sleeping in the middle of the day. I pulled away from Bree carefully so as not to wake her, and pulled the light cover up to her waist. I went into the head and relieved myself, and yes, I did wash my hands. Then I went up onto the deck to find out what time it was and to see if there was anything going on.

The sun was just starting to set, so we had been asleep for quite a while. My tongue felt fuzzy and my head was a pounding lump of wet clay. How much did we have to drink anyway? The afternoon was all a blur at the moment, but I did remember that it was Caleb who had given us a steady flow of alcohol. This fact served to increase my distrust and dislike of him.

I observed Marissa clutching at a rail and vomiting noisily over the side of the ship and into the water. A cackle that I recognized came from behind me and I cringed. Of course Caleb would be enjoying the sight of something like this.

"She's feedin' the fish. Chunky style." He was such an odious, foul person, but his words made me gag loud enough for him to hear me. "Why don't you go join her, Justin? Plenty of fish to feed y'know."

He was still drunk as well. "Why don't you just shut up for once? Just once? This is all your fault you know?" It surprised me when he did shut up, and wandered toward the other end of the ship. I went over to Marissa and put a hand on her shoulder. I then asked what had to be the most ridiculous question of all time, "Are you okay?"

She shook her head in the negative, and proceeded to make some additional retching dry-heave noises. I again fought back the bile rising in my own throat, and knelt down beside her. There was a towel on the rail from when they had all been swimming earlier, and I handed it to her.

"Water … please." She croaked. I hurried down below and grabbed a bottle of Aquafina for her. On my return trip I unscrewed the cap and then passed the bottle to her. She took it with trembling hands, spilled a bit, and then drank noisily. Some water ran over her chin and down the sculptured curve of her throat. "Thank you, Justin."

"No big deal. How's Jaffe feeling?" I glanced over toward their ship, the *Marshall,* but there was not anyone else in sight.

"He's sleeping it off below. Neither one of us ever usually drinks that much. I'm sorry you had to see me like this," she added wiping again at her mouth. "Where's Bree?"

"She's below still sleeping as well. I'm glad I was here to help you."

Marissa took my hand in hers and squeezed. In what I interpreted as a suggestive voice, she said, "Thank you again." She raised a coquettish eyebrow, "I owe you one."

We stood, still holding hands, and I was wondering if I was reading too much into this or not. Of course I would never act on it if she were. I would never do anything to hurt Bree or to jeopardize our relationship. I slowly withdrew my hand from hers. "Like I said, no problem."

Dinner that evening was light, and there certainly was not any alcohol involved for Bree, Jaffe, Marissa, and myself. Not that we ate all that much, either. Caleb however, had several bottles of beer throughout dinner.

"You're really knocking those things back," I observed.

He eyed me for a long moment before replying, "My doctor told me to drink plenty of fluids. Health reasons, ya know." Not content to leave it at that, he added, "At least I can handle my alcohol. Unlike you and your barf-buddy … all cozied up on the deck, today." He nodded toward Marissa. Even though it had been harmless, we both blushed with embarrassment. Bree and Jaffe had quizzical looks on their faces. For some reason, I felt the need to explain.

"She was throwing up over the side earlier," I think this only embarrassed her more, for she lowered her head. "I brought her a towel … and water." Even I heard how lame that sounded, and I knew that Marissa and I would have some explaining to do later to Bree and Jaffe. I again felt a surge of anger, and wondered where the M-4 was. I had never thought of myself as a violent person, I guess Caleb brought out the worst in me. So ended our second day at sea.

The next morning was another cookie-cutter beautiful day. The temperature was in the low eighties, the sky blue, and the water warm. Everyone got along well and even Caleb seemed to be on his best behavior early on. Late morning, and Jaffe, Marissa, Bree, and I all went snorkeling on a nearby coral reef. The fish were all the colors of the rainbow, as were the different types of coral. The water itself was a startling shade of blue, mirroring the sky overhead. The corals ranged in colors from shades of green, to reds, whites, and yellows. They were all sorts of fantastic shapes including fans, finger-like structures, corals that looked like melted candles, flat domes, rounded areas, and on and on. It was a veritable feast for the eyes. I was sure that if my mother had been there, she would have been able to identify all the types of coral, as well as the abundant marine life.

Bree and Marissa were both wearing bikinis which was a pleasant distraction from our underwater sight seeing trip. Not that I was looking, but I did notice that Marissa also had her naval pierced, as well as a circular tattoo in the small of her back. My mask kept fogging up, so I rose to the surface to clear it out. Caleb had suggested we spit into our masks to adjust the temperature of the glass to our faces. The thought of my own saliva on my face for some reason had disgusted me, so I had ignored his advice. I was paying for it now.

The others surfaced beside me and we decided to swim back to the ship. Bree and I held hands as we swam, which was nice. I could feel the big dopey grin on my face, and I think that even with Caleb in the picture, it was still one of the happiest moments of my life.

Back on board the ship, the girls went to work on their tans, while the three of us fished for lunch. Of course Caleb had to regale Jaffe with the shark incident, playing up his part in it, and making the shark larger than I remembered it being. I was just thankful that our fearless leader seemed to be maintaining his composure today, and was abstaining from alcohol. So far, so good. At one point, Jaffe nudged me and nodded toward the stern of the ship where the girls were. They were both lying on their stomachs, but had undone the strings to their tops. I grinned foolishly, feeling like a teenaged boy with his first crush. I guess that is the best way to describe being in love. Anything and everything is possible. Your whole life is in front of you, and you always have unlimited energy for everything. My thoughts were interrupted by a tug on my line. For the next several minutes I thought only of landing the fish I had hooked.

Caleb cleaned and grilled our catch. To drink we had lots of ice water. Lunch was light and we made pleasant conversation. We found out more about Jaffe and Marissa, and shared details of our lives with them. We even made plans for getting together once we all made it back to the states. Thankfully, Caleb remained on good behavior. Perhaps he felt guilty about past sins, and was trying to make amends. It was also possible that even he was able to feel some of the animosity the rest of us had been directing his way as of late.

After lunch everyone napped for a while, and then applied copious amounts of sun screen before we spent the rest of the afternoon frolicking in the sun. There was more swimming, a brief bout of snorkeling, and a half-hearted attempt to fish again. It was not a long day, but it had been a busy one, a good one. As Bree and I dropped off to sleep that night, very aware that Caleb was sleeping on the deck above us, I realized that the proverbial clock was ticking on my mission. It also dawned on me that tomorrow we would probably go our separate ways as well.

The following day was a veritable repeat of the day before. The difference was, and it remained unspoken for most of the day, was that we all needed to continue on in our journeys. Again the absence of alcohol was noticeable, although Caleb did have one bottle of beer with lunch. The rest of us had politely declined. After we had eaten, all five of us sat in silence and stared out at the waves and at the forlorn island.

Jaffe broke the silence at last, "We're thinking of heading out for the Bahamas this afternoon." My head bobbled like one of the cheap toys. "Why don't you guys join us?"

At first I thought he meant switch to their ship, but there was not enough room. Then I realized what he had meant. I glanced at Bree who was giving me an encouraging smile. Caleb had been right, there was not much of anything out here. Yet I still felt … obligated to at least try for a little longer to find Erich Craigie.

"Give Caleb your heading an we'll join you in a couple of days. The *Madora* is faster than your lobster boat anyway. We'll probably be waiting for you at Nassau."

Jaffe feigned insult. "Lobster boat? The *Marshall* is a custom yacht, the talk of the seven seas! Unlike your garbage scow."

"Hey, Caleb growled, "Yer talkin' 'bout my ship."

The light banter continued and too soon we were saying our farewells. Caleb shook hands with Marissa and Jaffe, Bree kissed both of them. I shook Jaffe's hand warmly, and Marissa kissed both of my cheeks.

As they were sailing off, Jaffe called back, "See you in a couple of days!"

We stood there waving, and I had one arm around Bree. Everyone was smiling and happy. I wish now we had sailed with them. Bree, Caleb, and I never made it to the Bahamas.

CHAPTER 7

▼

We also got underway soon after Marissa and Jaffe had left. There really was not any reason for us to stay in the area any longer, and without our friends it seemed lonely. We passed several atolls which were extremely small islands. One of them was so small that it would have barely held both Bree and myself comfortably at the same time. We anchored around a larger island for a late lunch, and then Bree and I rowed ashore to do some exploring. We walked a couple of the beaches hand in hand looking for Turnip Whelk shells without any real hope for success.

Later that afternoon, another larger island appeared on the horizon. I directed Caleb's attention to it, to see what he thought. He raised the binoculars to his eyes and gave it a long critical look. Then he glanced down at his watch.

"Kinda early to be stoppin' fer the day, ain't it?"

"It's just for a bit. Bree and I ..." I paused, trying to derive a plausible excuse that he would believe. "We need a little—alone time."

"Ohh," he winked conspiratorially. "I gotcha. A little a—lone time." He stretched it out, making it sound like something dirty. The facade of two male sexist pigs bonding was complete. He turned the ship in the direction of the island.

We made decent time and were soon anchored off the eastern shore of the island. I scanned the shoreline for any vestiges of human inhabitation. Not finding any, Bree and I then lowered the smaller boat and rowed to the shore. We rowed figuring that we needed the exercise. We pulled our small craft up on the beach so that it would not be washed away by the waves.

"What did you tell Caleb?" She asked, itching a spot where she had burned and was now peeling. Bree was very fair skinned, and despite using a strong sun block with a high SPF, she had darkened easily in the constant strong sun. It had not taken long for her to become very dark. She reminded me of a copper penny.

I grinned. "I simply explained to him that you and I needed some a— lone time."

She laughed and recognized at once who I was imitating. "Do we?" I put my arms around her and kissed her. An hour later, and after further exploration of the island, we made our way back to the dingy.

I turned and looked at the dense undergrowth. "Should we try inland?"

Bree wrinkled her nose in thought. "I don't know. It looks kind of thick in there."

I nodded. "Yeah, you're probably right. No sense in getting all torn up for a wild goose chase anyway."

"It's not a wild goose chase, Justin. It's important to you. Therefore, it's important to me. Besides," she added mischievelously, "Aren't I usually right all the time, anyway?"

"No comment," I replied. It had been a rhetorical question.

As we were getting into the smaller water craft, Bree playfully kicked water at me.

"Don't start something you can't finish." I cautioned her. Ignoring my warning, she splashed me again. "Last chance …" She lowered her eyes in a seductive manner and looked up at me. "Alright, alright. Get in, let's get going, already."

"You're beginning to sound like Caleb," she observed in a dry voice.

"In order to sound like Caleb I would have to get a lobotomy, drop my IQ by half, and be a raging alcoholic most of the time."

Even I heard the harsh tone in my voice. I was too busy trying to row us out into deeper water so that I could start the engine to have time or breath to apologize. Judging that we were out far enough, I shipped the oars and pulled on the starter cord. The engine sputtered, did not even come close to turning over, and died.

"Um, Justin?" I did not answer. We were now caught in a cross current that was running parallel to the shore. We were inexorably being pulled away from the island and the *Madora*. I almost instantly regretted not bringing a walkie-talkie or cell phone so that we could communicate with Caleb. If wishes were fishes, we would have an ocean full. I know, not funny.

I yanked hard on the starter cord. The engine again sputtered, coughed, offered a tantalizing hope of starting, and then died. The stinging smell of gas filled the air. I had flooded the engine. I cursed in a loud voice and slapped the engine with the side of my hand. I tried to start it one more time, but the slap had not helped either. Not that I had thought that it would.

"We'll just do it the old-fashioned way," I told her. Trying to muster as much confidence in my voice as I was able to. I sat and pulled at the oars for several minutes, but it was a losing battle. We were drifting farther away by the second.

Bree stood up and cupped her hands around her mouth in order to amplify her voice, "Caleb! Help!"

Regretting that we needed to rely on him to rescue us, and that he would never let me forget it, I felt a momentary twinge of embarrassment. I have never been a big water person, but even I knew enough to not stand up in a boat. "Bree …" I did not have time to finish. A wave rocked the boat causing her to lose her balance. I watched aghast as in slow motion my fiancee tumbled overboard with a loud splash.

I turned and lunged toward her outstretched hand. Our fingers brushed briefly, and then she was behind me. "Hold on, Bree!" I pulled hard on the right oar, trying to turn the boat around. She was calmly treading water with a droll look on her face, almost as if she could not believe that she had fallen overboard. She was bobbing on the surface not fifteen feet away from me. Then I saw the fin.

I used to laugh at the cartoons when their eyes would bulge in excitement or fear. I literally felt my own eyes grow wide in their sockets, and I knew without any doubt that I would never laugh at those cartoons again. My mouth was as dry as the sandy beach we had crossed minutes ago. I pulled hard on the oars, watching Bree who was oblivious to the fins, over my shoulder.

A second and third fin joined the first. I was not sure how close they were to Bree, too close. They wavered for a moment in the waves, and then turned in her direction. Two more good pulls on the oars and I was coming up beside her. The fins were closing in as well. I had seen enough shark movies to know what to expect. I was already visualizing it with my eyes open.

She reached up an outstretched hand so that I could help her out of the water. I would have one chance, and one chance only at getting her onboard before the sharks got to her. Without any hesitation on my part, I reached past her wet slippery hand, and latched firmly onto her wrist in a vice-like grip I was sure hurt. I saw the surprise and indignation on her face as I dug my nails in so that she would not slip. Without any warning, ceremony, or preamble, I yanked hard, pulling her into the boat and on top of me. There was a loud thump and a yell of pain as her leg hit the metal side of the boat.

"Justin! That hurt! Why did you pull so hard?" Not only was there anger in her voice, but also surprise. I had never been rough with her like that before, not even in jest.

"There are—sharks," I gasped in relief, now that she was safe. I squeezed her close to me, hard. I exhaled and could feel the own pounding of my heart. I sat up and pointed at the three fins which had by now moved past us and were swimming aimlessly away.

They vanished for a moment, and then reappeared, swimming in formation. Bree chuckled and took my face in her hands. "Those aren't sharks, Justin. They're dolphins. See the hooked dorsal fins?"

"The what?" I sat up more as well. The fins were still there, moving back and forth.

"The top fin that sticks out of the water. It's called the dorsal fin. On dolphins it's hooked, and on sharks it's triangular. Don't you watch Animal Planet?"

I gritted my teeth together. Obviously I did not watch enough television. I turned back to the engine, daring it not to start, and gave it a good, hard yank. This time it coughed to life, and stayed running. Ten minutes later we were reunited with Caleb. He raised his eyebrows and looked down at his watch before observing,

"That was a lot of alone time."

I was inclined to agree. I waved him off dismissively, "Yeah, yeah. Save it." But dear, sweet Bree decided to tell him about the dolphins. This caused a great deal of laughter, all at my expense. I was unable to see the humor in the situation. I had been terrified that I was going to lose the only woman I had ever truly loved in front of my very eyes. I realized again how small this boat—that is right, boat, was. I wished again that we had just stayed home. Caleb kept mumbling to himself about dolphins and sharks, and then would burst into merry peals of laughter. I finally told him to shut up, among other things. This seemed to work, because he set a new record of almost two hours of silence. We moored around a small island for the night.

Bree and I sat on the deck with our legs dangling over the side and watched the moon and stars. Waves slapped rhythmically against the ship which still retained some warmth from the afternoon sun. She snuggled in closer to my shoulder, and I kissed the top of her head.

She broke the silence with an abrupt question, "Are we still planning on following Jaffe and Marissa in a couple of days?"

I nodded, but even I could hear the resignation in my voice, "Even though it's not much, we'll check this island tomorrow, and then I'll have Caleb set a course for the Bahamas."

I felt her head move in agreement against my shoulder. "That sounds good. Are you … disappointed we didn't find Erich Craigie?"

There was a loud bang from below as Caleb dropped something, followed by the sounds of his muted curses. We both jumped, startled. I knew he was impatient as well about going to the Bahamas. Although I feared what would happen if he had that much access to the bars.

"This trip is supposed to be about more than just finding my real father." I said in the most tactful way that I could. "We've never really had a lot of alone time, although with Captain Caleb around, I guess we still don't."

Bree looked toward the island, judging its distance. "Do you want to paddle over to the island tonight? Just the two of us?"

I smiled in the dark. "What, and face those man-eating dolphins again?"

"I'm sorry about that, Justin. You do have to admit though, it was kind of funny."

"It wasn't at the time. I was terrified that I would lose you. Although," I admitted reluctantly, "I guess I can see the humor in it now."

"Speaking of now, you still haven't responded to my proposal."

"I'll tell you what, you go grab a couple of blankets, and I'll go get the rowboat ready, and we'll paddle over to the shore for a while." So we did.

The next morning dawned cloudy and cool. The sky was a flat gray, with storm clouds on the horizon. Bree and I had spent much of the night on the beach, but the noises emanating from the dark woods and an overly inquisitive sand crab and eventually chased us back to the ship. The three of us ate breakfast in relative silence. Silence was always relative when Caleb was around. Although he was a bit miffed at us for rowing over to the island the night before and not telling him about it. If making him angry was the only way to keep him quiet, I started devising a plethora of ways to keep him mad for the rest of the trip.

"Bree and I were thinking of exploring the island a bit, this morning."

Caleb did not seem surprised. "What? You guys need that much alone time?"

I bit back my original response which would have been about needing time away from him, and instead replied, "We'll be back in less than an hour. After that, we can head for the Bahamas and catch up with Jaffe and Bree. If that's okay with you?"

"Sweet! Now you're talking! Oh, man, have you ever been to the Bahamas?" I shook my head in the negative. "Y'all in for a real treat, then! Sparkling sand, clear water, parties going on twenty-four/seven. It's like Mardi Gras, Carnivale, and Christmas all in one!"

Somehow I doubted that. Instead, I nodded, wanting to keep him in a good mood. I stood up, stretched, and looked in Bree's direction. "Ready?" I asked, and she gave me a thumbs up.

She slid back in her deck chair and also stood. Today she was wearing a maroon windbreaker over a navy blue tank top with khaki shorts. Her hair was pulled back in a loose ponytail which accentuated the curve of her neck and throat. She did not have on any jewelry except for two small pearl earrings which I had given her for Christmas last year, and of course, her engagement ring. I loved her so much, and my heart swelled with pride at the thought that she had agreed to spend the rest of her life with me.

I checked the engine as we got into the smaller boat. I did not want a repeat of the scene from the day before when it had not started. I did not let myself think too much about what could have happened. We also had remembered to bring along one of the two-way radios this time as well. Caleb had also promised to keep an eye out for us this time, in light of our previous experience. I again left my pistol and M-4 on board. To be honest, I had the M-4 beneath our bed, wedged between two suitcases, and it was loaded. Bree did not know this, but it made me feel safer for some odd reason. Safer from what unknown and unnamed danger I was unsure, but I had been sleeping better at night.

On our way over we chatted about the weather, and the Bahamas, and reuniting with Marissa and Jaffe. Once at the beach we tied off the smaller craft, and walked along, glancing now and then at the sand. We did not have much hope of finding a Turnip Whelk, and if we had, it would not have proven anything conclusive. But Bree did find a Sand Dollar, whole and undamaged in any way. It was flat, white, circular, and filled her palm. It looked kind of like the top crust for an apple pie, and there were five small slits in it. I did not know that much about them, but I knew enough that finding a whole one was very rare.

"A good luck souvenir of our trip," quipped Bree, and I smiled and nodded in agreement.

As we walked part of the way around the island the sun came out and the sand grew hot to walk on. I glanced around for some landmarks before tugging Bree toward the dense growth that would offer some shade and a respite from the sun.

"Are you kidnaping me?" She asked in a facetious tone of voice.

"Well, my father was supposedly a pirate ..." I let the last word hang as we stepped off the beach and into the trees. My train of thought vanished as I realized that there was a relatively clear cut path in front of us. "Shall we?" I gestured toward the trail, making a sweeping display with my hand.

"I'm not sure we should. We'd be out of sight of the ship."

"I'll protect you, don't worry." I put as much gallantry into my voice as possible.

She smiled up at me, a trusting look on her face, and gave my hand a squeeze. "My hero," she responded with a mock swoon.

"And you're mine," I answered without any hesitation at all.

It was cooler, and the feathery palms and other trees made an almost completely enclosed canopy over our heads. There was thick brush on both sides of the sandy path. Coconuts lay scattered about, reminding me for some morbid reason of human skulls. There was not much for the auditory senses to pick up. The constant soft moan of the wind, and an occasional bird chirped in the forest. I also noticed sporadic flashes of brown and green as geckos or some other type of lizard would dart off to safety. A gust of wind caused the trees above us to whisper softly, almost like human voices.

"This is kind of creepy," observed Bree.

"I don't know," I paused for dramatic effect. "I think it's kind of romantic."

"You would," she answered, trying not to laugh at the huskiness in my voice.

I pulled her toward me, took her face gently in my hands, and kissed her hard on the mouth. "You're insatiable," she said with a giggle. Before I could respond, or further my advances, the radio on my hip crackled and Caleb muttered something. "Don't answer it," she murmured, kissing my neck. I slid the strap of her tank top over and kissed her bare shoulder.

"Hey, kids," came Caleb's clear voice over the radio, effectively killing the moment. "I hate to interrupt your a—lone time," he made the last two words sound dirty somehow, "But we got a storm comin' in, an' I need y'all back here, pronto." Bree rolled her eyes and stepped back from our embrace. Caleb seemed to have a knack for ruining things.

I unclipped the radio from my hip, and responded, "I hear you, Caleb. We're on our way." I gave my fiancee a quick kiss on the cheek, "To be continued," I said, trying to placate her. Or maybe it was myself I was trying to placate.

We made it back to the beach and our boat without any problems. Caleb was right, another storm was brewing. The sky had filled with storm clouds and the wind had picked up. It was also starting to sprinkle. Being otherwise occupied, and sheltered by the trees overhead, we had failed to notice this while we had been in the woods.

Bree glanced at the rising waves, which had turned a dark gray color. "This isn't going to be much fun, is it?" Instead of replying which would have only wasted time, I handed her a life jacket which she put on without further conversation. I also strapped on one, and although it did not look like it would keep a cat afloat, I knew appearances were deceiving.

The engine started, and although the water was a bit rough, we made it back to the *Madora* without further incident. Caleb was busy tying things down, and tending to the sails, which he was in the process of lowering and securing. He glanced up at us as we climbed on board. "You got here,"

"Just in time," I finished for him. "I've heard it a thousand times, Caleb."

"I know, but I couldn't help myself." Turning businesslike, he continued, "PFDs at all times and tether lines too. I'm not sure how bad this one is gonna get."

"Can't we just take shelter on the other side of the island? It's large enough isn't it?"

"Not that I have time to argue with you, but this island runs east-west, same direction as the storm is runnin'. We'd get blasted if we stayed here. We're gonna try and outrun it."

Remembering how well that worked the last time, I went below with Bree. We traded our life vests for the heavier, more durable PFDs with water activated strobes. If I had only known beforehand that sailing was going to be like this …

"How about next time we go somewhere, we fly?" I asked Bree, and she nodded without hesitation. She was as adventurous and as daring as I was, but this was getting a bit ridiculous. "I'm going to go up and see if Caleb needs any help." I turned to go and she clutched at my hand, squeezing it hard enough to hurt.

"Justin?" I turned and looked back at her. "Be careful, okay?"

"You know me," I replied. "I always am."

"That's what worries me."

I gave her a quick kiss and then headed for the stairs which lead up to the deck. "Come on, Bree, my middle name is careful." I said over my shoulder to her.

"No, it's not. It's Allen. And don't forget, I'm still planning on being Mrs. Justin Allen Thyme, so be careful."

I secured the hatch behind me and reached for a tether line. I attached it, and then double checked the harness. The last time I had been on the deck during a storm, I had been very fortunate. I was not going to take any chances, especially with the future Mrs. Justin Thyme waiting for me below. Holding on to the rail, I made my way back to where Caleb was sitting at the wheel.

The wind had increased in strength, and it was raining for real now. The waves were a mirror of the sky, and the thunder reminded me of the noise in a busy bowling alley. Even the air seemed to be a wet gray, occasionally brightened by a flash of lightening. I stumbled on the slick rain-washed deck, and Caleb grabbed me by the arm, steadying me.

"How's it going?" I had to yell to be overheard above the storm.

"Another freakin' day in paradise! Man, I can not wait to get to Bermuda!"

"Are we having fun yet?" A wave slammed into the side of the ship and I grabbed the rail.

"Oh, yeah. This sucks like a vacuum. We won't hafta worry about this kinda crap once we get to the tropics." He wiped rain or wave water from his face. "We were at about twenty lat, thirty longe before this hit. Now, I'm not so sure. The wind and the waves have prolly pushed us to the south and west. We'll get our bearings once we get outta this soup or find a sheltered cove." By lat and longe I assumed he meant latitude and longitude. Although I knew the terms from geography, they did not mean a whole lot to me at this moment in time. Caleb gripped the wheel in a tight, vice-like grip, and spun it so that we were now facing into the waves.

This storm did not seem as severe as the last one, but I was not going to underestimate it. Two things I had learned out here were that appearances were deceiving, and to never take anything for granted. We were in the Bermuda Triangle, and this place was notorious for strange occurrences and disappearances. I did not plan on being added to the lists of lost ships or missing souls. I kept my eyes opened and on the lookout for errant waves. Visibility, while lessened because of the rain and waves, was still decent. I could see close to seventy yards in every direction.

Caleb spat a mouthful of saltwater toward the rail. "Man, I could go for a beer …"

I nodded, and to be polite, contributed, "I've been dreaming about ice cream, myself."

"Really? Oh, crap!" We averted our faces as a wave broke over the port side. "I've got some Ben and Jerry's Heath Bar Crunch down in the freezer. I've been savin' it for a special occasion." A loud clap of thunder interrupted our conversation. We both ducked.

"You just bought my soul, Caleb." Bree and I had always favored the Vermont ice cream company which also had a conscience. The Ben and Jerry's Ice Cream Company practiced environmentally friendly methods, bought local milk, donated to non-profit organizations, as well as other philanthropist endeavors.

"There," Caleb nodded toward our aft. In the distance was a clump of trees made hazy by the rain. "It's a pretty ratty lookin' excuse for an island, but if it gets us outta the wind and waves, we'll take it."

Under steady and reliable power from our engines, we motored toward the land. Caleb also kept a close eye on our depth finder. It was not uncommon for the water depths to change drastically over a short distance. I shuddered to think about what could happen to us if we ran aground in a storm like this, regardless of the proximity of land. I also did not relish the idea of the three of us plus supplies in the motorboat trying to navigate through the storm.

Fortunately, we were able to reach the lee side of the island in relative safety. Caleb idled the engines until after I had dropped the large anchor overboard, and then lowered a secondary anchor over the stern to keep us pointed in the right direction. Combined, the two weights would keep us stationary, which would prevent us from beaching on the shore or running aground.

"Three fathoms of water underneath us," Caleb informed me. "That's almost twenty feet of water, so we should be okay for now."

The two of us scrambled around the deck double checking to make sure that everything was tied down and secure. The storm had not abated much. It was still raining, the wind was still blowing, and thunder threatened to deafen us while lightening illuminated the gloom. Perhaps I was becoming inured to the weather. I did not feel like every single bolt was going to strike me, now. I was also becoming accustomed to being constantly soaked. I wondered if my toes were becoming webbed. The waves, however, were not as large, and more importantly, we felt safe. Speaking from a psychological point of view, that was key.

"We're safer than if you were in your momma's arms!" Chortled Caleb. I somehow doubted that. Nor did I wish to go into details about my family, especially my mother. I did not argue, however, as I was just as relieved as he was to find this sanctuary. He tapped the compass and I looked over his shoulder in time to see it spinning in a most erratic manner.

"No worries," he confided in me. "Happens alla time in the Triangle. Most compasses point to the Magnetic North, but in some places down here they point True North instead."

"What's the difference?" I asked intrigued. I had read about the strange effect the Bermuda Triangle had on compasses, but I had forgotten what it said. I had been preoccupied more with the pirate side of my research. I did remember that the peculiar behavior with compasses also happened in only one other known place in the world, and that was Japan.

"For us, here? Not much. But out in the wide open ocean without landmarks, we would be talkin' twenty-plus degrees—which is a lot. It's easy to get lost around here, but you don't have anything to worry about. That's why you hired me. I'm your freakin' guardian angel."

Not exactly the analogy I was thinking. In an offhanded tone of voice I asked, "What about pirates?" While I waited for an answer I busied myself by checking the lashing on a sail.

"I told you before. There. Are. No. Pirates. I've been sailin' around here for years and I've never seen that Johnny Depp guy once."

"I'm talking about modern-day pirates. You should see what I found on the internet."

His face split into a lecherous grin. "You oughta see what I found on the internet. You're talkin' crap 'bout pirates, anyway. We're fine up here for now. Why don't you go below and rustle up some grub and a pot of hot coffee?"

"Aye, aye, Captain." I gave him a facetious salute, and went below to follow orders.

I checked on Bree, first. I believe the polite terminology was that she was a bit green around the gills. This surprised me, because during the first storm she had not become seasick.

"Are you okay, hon?"

She nodded, and blotted at her mouth with a towel. "Yeah. My stomach has just been bothering me as of late, that's all. How are things going up top? Did I hear the anchors go?"

"Everything's fine. I've got to make dinner and coffee tonight, Captain Blood's orders."

The implication of what she had said was lost on me at that time. I promptly forgot our conversation, dismissing her upset stomach as a product of the rolling waves, and moved on to the next order of business. I do not think that if I had pursued that line of thought that it would have changed what happened later, but sometimes I find myself wondering. I also do not think that even Bree truly knew or accepted it. We had talked about having children, someday. Like so many other things in my life, that too, never came to pass.

Bree and I made dinner together on the small stove in the galley. I dropped one of the hamburgers on the floor and we both laughed like little children. I acted like I was going to spit in Caleb's coffee mug, and we laughed even harder.

The waters were still rough, so we ate below. Caleb and I had both changed into dry clothes before we ate. Dinner was a quiet affair, and I never did see any hint of the Ben and Jerry's ice cream which he had alluded to earlier. Typical of Caleb, was all I thought.

Perhaps it was the weather, or the fact that we were in the Bermuda triangle that caused the sense of foreboding in me. I have never professed to any clairvoyant abilities, and I could not quite put a finger on what was leading to my feeling that way, but it was there. While Bree was in the bathroom taking her evening shower, I knelt down and rooted beneath the bed. I removed the case containing the M-4, and casting a furtive glance over my shoulder in the direction of the sound of the running shower water, I proceeded to open the case.

The M-4 had an oily, flat-black sheen about it. The patina was caused by the protective layer of oil I had rubbed onto it after Caleb and I had fired it that one time. I sighed, and removed the weapon, sliding a clip into place with an audible click. I pushed the box back beneath the bed, and then wedged the gun between two pillows underneath as well. I was trying to remember where I had put the Glock pistol I had bought from RJ when Bree called from the shower,

"I need a handsome lifeguard to wash my back ... Will you go get Caleb?"

I did not bother to reply. I instead chose to march toward our small, semi-private bathroom, and apply for the lifeguard position myself.

I awoke the next morning to relative silence. The storm had ended. I could not get over the weather extremes in this area. Nor could I quite reconcile the fact that the storms would arise without warning. Why would anyone in their right minds want to live in this part of the world? Still, it had been my idea to travel this way, so I had only myself to blame. I mentioned my opinion concerning the extremes in weather to Bree, and she had replied,

"If it wasn't for the bad days, we wouldn't appreciate the good ones." I could not argue with the logic of that. Bree was an eternal optimist; it was just one more thing that I loved about her. She could always find the silver lining in every storm cloud. Every day was full of infinite possibilities for good things to happen, and she left the misfortunes of the day before behind her.

I remember an horrific ice storm our second year in college. We were without power for three days, and a large ice encrusted branch had smashed the rear window in Bree's Honda. It had been early in our relationship, we had been dating for probably all of two weeks at that point. We had decided to go for a walk when the storm was over to survey the other damage. Holding hands and balancing on the precarious surface that was in places an inch thick with ice, we had stumbled and slid down the sidewalk, amazed at what we were seeing. Instead of being overwhelmed by the destruction all around us as I had been, what I remember most was Bree's voice filled with the awe and wonder of a child saying, "It's beautiful. It looks like everything is encased in glass."

I shook away the memory, and tore my gaze away from the small window/porthole we had been peering through. We got dressed and went up onto the deck to find Caleb surveying the ship with his hands on his hips.

"Well, kids," how ingratiating, I thought. He was not that much older than we were. "Looks like we made it through 'nother one. I want to double check everything, though, just in case. "It'll be about an hour—hour an' a half tops. This time Wednesday and we'll be in the Bahamas! Wait'll y'all see the bars in Nassau!"

Bree and I gave each other a long, knowing look. If we had wanted bars we could have stayed at home, or taken a vacation in New Orleans. Not only would there have been the social scene of Bourbon Street, but there was also the added attraction of the rich history of the French Quarter.

Also, Anne Rice, one of my favorite authors, lived there. Many of her novels were set in the south. I remembered a college professor always admonishing us to 'write what you know about.' Advice I planned on giving my own students someday.

A group of my male friends and I had all gone to Mardi Gras our freshman year in college. I had been amazed at the size of the crowds, the sheer numbers of human bodies packed into small areas. I remember our endless quest for beads, and some of our embarrassing methods of obtaining them. The mind numbing amount of alcohol consumed, as well as the debauchery we saw in the streets had shocked me. It was supposed to be a religious holiday, or so I had assumed. The one image that sticks with me still, is that of a beautiful brunette in a wheelchair up on a balcony tossing beads to the screaming masses. She and I had made eye contact, and with an elegant flick of her wrist, she had launched a string of plastic beads in my direction.

Caleb interrupted my thoughts. "Say, why don't you two motor on over to that island and find us some fresh coconuts? After that wind, they'll be all over the ground. I'll make my famous Poached Chicken in Coconut Curry Sauce for lunch today." He paused, musing something over in his mind that probably had something to do with alcohol. "Maybe we'll do a theme lunch. I know a bunch of mixed drinks you can make with coconut milk, too." The joys of being right. I did not congratulate myself too much however, Caleb was predictable that way.

I shrugged, so Bree and I prepared to go over to the island. I helped her down into the motorboat, and wonder of wonders, the engine started immediately.

"It must be our lucky day," I observed with a sardonic grin. Caleb offered a walkie-talkie, and I waved him off. This was going to be a quick trip. The Bahamas were waiting.

We made it to the opposite shore without incident, tied off the boat, and proceeded to walk hand in hand along the beach. We proceeded a little way into the jungle, watching the ground for promising coconuts. There was a small sandy clearing, and chatting all the while, it did not take long for us to each pick up several green and brown coconuts the size of footballs.

"This one looks like Caleb," I laughed at Bree's observation. I was about to say something witty of my own, in regards to the way she was holding the coconuts clutched to her chest, when I heard a stick snap in the forest behind us. This was followed by a muttered curse that I recognized came from a human voice. It had been the sound a stick makes when you step on it, and there was no mistaking the swear. We were not alone on this island.

CHAPTER 8

"Well, well, well," a voice that reminded me of someone who had gargled with gravel rasped from behind us. "What do we have here?" I put a protective arm in front of Bree, a weak shield, but it was better than not having anything at all. There was an audible click which I recognized as the trigger of a pistol being pulled back in preparation of being fired. "Don't try anythin' stupid, now. Jest turn 'round, real nice an' easy like, an' keep your hands where we can see 'em."

I felt Bree tense up beside me, the urge for fight or flight was strong, but we complied with the request. Standing in a semi-circle behind us were four scrawny, ratty dressed men. They had long scraggily hair and beards, and their clothes were torn and shabby. Looking very out of place in their hands was an odd assortment of weapons, all pointed at us. I recognized an M-4, similar to my own, as well as another assault rifle, a hunting rifle, and a pistol.

"Hm," said the largest of the four. His voice was the same one that had initially spoken. It did not take a great stretch of imagination to assume that he was the leader of this scruffy band. "Ain't you jest the cutest couple?" It was a rhetorical question, so we did not answer him.

"Erich?" One of them blurted out. Surprised I turned and looked at him with the same look of amazement that he was giving me. "It can't be. But you're the spittin' image ..."

"Shut up!" Snarled the leader. He looked down at the half dozen coco-nuts we had been carrying and had dropped when he had ordered us to raise our hands. "What're you doin' here on our island? We don't like visi-tors." His eyes never left my face.

Bree responded, "We're just passing through. There are eight of our friends on our ship waiting for us, and ..."

"Right." The leader cut her off. He rolled the word off his tongue, drenching it with as much sarcasm as he could. "Eight, huh? We counted the two of you and one other doofus on your little sailboat. So don't gimme any of that eight crap."

It had been a good attempt to bluff our way out of this, I will give her that. My attention was still on the man who had spoken my father's name. It was difficult to determine his age. He could have been anywhere from forty to sixty. I made eye contact with him and asked,

"Did you know a man named Erich Craigie?"

The surprise was even more evident on his face. "Know 'im? I ..."

"I tole you to shet yer trap." Broke in the leader. "I ast the questions 'round here. Got it?" I nodded and he went on, "How do you know the name Erich Craigie?"

Without thinking first, I answered, "He was my father. Did you know him as well?"

One of the others muttered an expletive, and the M-4 came up from his hip to his shoulder in one fluid movement and was now pointed directly at me. I tried to swallow.

"You could say we're familiar wid da name. Seein' as how introductions ain't been made yet, my name is Russ." He nodded at the man who had confused me with my father. "This's Rob." He looked at the other two who were cookie-cutter ugly. "An' these two gents are Blu an' Carlos. Erich Craigie was really yer father, huh?" I nodded. "Ya got a first name, Craigie?"

"It's Justin. My mother," I was interrupted before I could continue.

"Nik," said Rob. Russ whirled on him and backhanded him, causing him to fall to the ground. Everybody else stood frozen, watching this sec-ondary drama play out.

"One more word outta you big mouth, an' yer done." He looked at me, the rifle pointed in my direction. "Go ahead, Craigie, I can't wait to hear this."

"My mother married a man named Japhet Thyme when she got back to the states. Thinking I was his son, they married. I have his last name, not Erich's."

"You gotta be kiddin'?" Snorted Russ. "Justin Time? Boy, your parents musta hated you to saddle you with that name." I remained quiet. In high school, one of my team mates had been named Noah Zark Franklin. It had been a standing joke about which one of us had the funnier name. "So ya found out da troof, somehow, an' come out here lookin' for your real father?" Asked Russ. I nodded again, my arms starting to tire from keeping them raised. I tried to lower them and he snapped, "Arms up! Ain't dat da sweetest story you boys've heard in a while? Why ain't your mother along for the reunion?"

I had been going with blunt honesty thus far, and did not see any reason to change that strategy. We might still be able to talk our way out of this. I gave Russ an even look and responded, "She died in early May of this year of cervical cancer." Russ gave a grunt of what sounded like satisfaction, and Rob lowered his head and covered his eyes. They knew something, but what? "You knew my mother as well, I take it?"

Russ tensed up, and for a long moment I was sure that he was going to shoot me. His eyes narrowed and he growled, "You are so close to death, boy, you don't even know. I tole you, I ast da questions around here." He shifted the M-4 so that it was now pointing at Bree. I felt an involuntary widening of my eyes. "I need you. Her, I don't need. Next question outta you, an' she gets it. We clear?" I did not doubt him for a second on his threat.

"Crystal," I replied between clenched teeth, starting to doubt our ability to talk our way out of this situation. I did not dwell on other options, there were not any. As for the outcome of this chance meeting, I did not think about that too much either. It did not look good for us.

"We did know your mother," Russ responded. He nodded in Bree's direction. "An' who might this be?"

I did not appreciate the way he was undressing her with his eyes. In fact, all four of them were looking at her like hungry wolves stalking an injured, solitary sheep. I attempted to calculate the odds of getting a weapon from one of them and killing the others. Killing. It was my only option. Russ seemed to be a mind reader. Keeping the gun trained on Bree, but watching and speaking to me, he cautioned,

"Uh-uh. Don't even think it, Craigie. Now answer my question. Who's da girl?"

"My fiancee. Her name is Bree." I did not correct him about my last name.

"Great. We gots us a Justin Time, an' a girl named after some froggy cheese. What a world, what a world." He shook his head in disbelief. "So by some miracle, you find our island," noticing our trembling arms, he sighed and rolled his eyes. "Go ahead, put yer arms down, but don't try nothin'. So you find our island, and then we found you." He paused for a moment, thinking. "That solves a coupla our problems, but creates some too. It also makes fer one big problem fer you."

I held my tongue and gave him a quizzical look. He grinned without humor, and I noticed that both his front teeth were missing. The rest were yellowed nubs. "You're learnin'. We need a boat, you got one. Your boat is now my boat." I did not think Caleb was going to agree to that. Bree opened her mouth but my hand found hers and squeezed it in warning. "Da other person on yer boat ... is he armed?" I nodded and lowered my head. I felt for some strange reason like I had betrayed Caleb. I also was beginning to realize where this was all headed, and it was not good. I was not sure where the Glock was, but the M-4 was still loaded and beneath mine and Bree's bed. If I could get to it, we still might be able to get out of this. All three of us.

"Here's what we're gonna do," said Russ in an amiable, conversational tone of voice. "You an' I," he was staring at me, again. "Are gonna go out an' get your boat. Your pretty lil' fiancee," he sneered the word. "Is gonna stay here with my three friends to make sure you behave yourself. Once we have your boat, we'll drop you off in the shipping lane with the rowboat and enough supplies to last a coupla days. Nobody gets hurt." I could see in his small piggish eyes that almost everything he had said after the second sentence had been lies, and everyone present knew this.

Bree came to the same conclusion I had moments ago. "You're … you're pirates!"

"Aye, miss. That we are. But at the moment, we're between ships. A problem we're gonna solve here pretty quick." He glared at me. "Remember, no tricks," he gestured in Bree's direction. "Or you'll be needin' a new fiancee."

I nodded in acquiescence. I did not truly have any choice in the matter, and I was certainly not going to jeopardize Bree's safety if I could help it. Caleb's perhaps, but Bree, never. However, this was a no-win situation regardless of whether we cooperated or not.

Russ marched me back down to the beach to where we had dragged the dinghy up onto the shore and tied it to a palm tree. Before we stepped out onto the wide expanse of sand, he lifted a pair of battered binoculars to his eyes and looked in the direction of the *Madora*. Even with the naked eye I could not see any trace of Caleb. It was just our misfortune that he was probably napping below or something like that.

Russ and I entered the smaller boat after pushing it into the water. I sat in the front while he manned the motor. He kept the M-4 trained on me, with his finger resting on the trigger guard. From a distance of less than four feet, there was not any way that he would miss. Nor was there much of a chance for me to catch him off guard or to surprise him. If I attempted anything at all I did not doubt for a second that I would die a meaningless death. It was also a certainty that both Bree and Caleb would probably die as well. The pirates would still get the *Madora*. It was better to bide my time and wait for a more opportune moment to present itself.

We motored toward out ship in silence. I fidgeted a bit from the stress. Russ hissed a warning for me to sit still, and I did so. What he and the others had in mind exactly for us I was unsure, but it was probably not good. If they did let us go as they had implied they would, that would leave us as witnesses to what they had done. Also I still did not know the whereabouts of Erich Craigie. From the intonations of the pirates, it was a certainty that they knew something about him. It was my fervent hope that I would be able to discover exactly what they knew.

As we got to within ten feet of the *Madora*, Russ cut the engine. Our forward momentum brought us into contact with the hull of the larger ship with a slight bump and scraping noise. Caleb cursed from below and came stomping up onto the deck, cursing the entire way.

"Man, if you scraped the hull you can kiss your security deposit goodbye. I hope you found some ripe coconuts, the green ones will give you …" he noticed Russ. "Who're you?"

Instead of answering, Russ brought the M-4 up to shoulder level and squeezed off three quick rounds. I saw two of them hit Caleb. They knocked bloody, fist-sized holes in his chest. He stumbled backward, arms wind milling in a futile attempt to regain his balance. He backed into the rail that went around the ship, tumbled overboard vanishing from our sight, and landed with a loud, dull sounding splash. He probably died still not believing in pirates.

Russ gestured to the now empty deck, "After you." Figuring I was next to be shot, but powerless to do anything about it, I climbed on board the ship. Russ tossed me two mooring ropes and I tied the two ships together. "Back up," he ordered, and I took several steps back. The pirate then climbed up onto the deck and surveyed his new acquisition with a smug look of satisfaction on his scarred and twisted face.

"That was too easy," he gloated. "This is probably a quarter million dollar ship, an' now she's all mine." He took a deep breath, "It's good to be back on the water again."

"You didn't need to kill Caleb. That wasn't part of our deal."

He shrugged. "So I changed the deal. So what?"

"You probably didn't mean what you said about letting Bree and I go either, then." I made sure not to phrase it in the form of a question, keeping his earlier warning in mind.

"Look, kid, no offense, but yer dead weight. Your real father kept your mother around, and that's why he went down." I did not like the sound of that, nor the implications. He gestured with his left hand, "Now I would like fer you ta gimme a little tour of my new ship."

Refusing would have just brought about my death sooner. Instead, I was planning on what the best way to get him below and in the vicinity of my own M-4 was. Disposing of Russ was priority number one. Once that happened, I would go back to shore and pick off his friends from the jungle. Then Bree and I would get out of here as fast as the *Madora* could carry us. Caleb had shown me enough that I could run the engines and once safe, send out a distress call.

Russ and I walked around the top deck first. I pointed out equipment and its purpose to the best of my memory. He asked a lot of questions, most of which I could only offer vague answers to, despite his prodding. Several of his questions I was unable to answer at all, which lead to some frustration for both of us.

We went below and our first stop was Caleb's berth. I had only seen the inside of his room twice, and both times it had looked like a hurricane had passed through it. Things had not changed. There were clothes strewn across the floor, a few forlorn beer bottles rolled about on the floor, and what looked like a radio that he had taken apart was laying on a desk. Several dog-eared pictures were tacked to the wall. I assumed they were of his family.

We continued on to a quick inspection of the head, and the area where the engines were located. Here I did not have any acceptable answers to the questions Russ posed. I explained that we had chartered this ship, and not been active participants in the day-to-day operations and maintenance of it. Our room was last.

Bree had made the bed and had picked up a bit earlier this morning. It seemed like a lifetime ago, now, but it had been at the most only a couple of hours. Compared to Caleb's room, ours was immaculate. Bree had always been the meticulous one when it came to cleaning. I felt a bead of sweat run down from my hairline and over my jaw below my left ear. The moment of truth was drawing close. Russ kept one eye on me and the gun pointed in my direction. With his left hand he was opening random drawers and rooting around. He grunted in surprise when he discovered Bree's underwear drawer, and his attention momentarily was diverted away from me. This was the opportunity I had been waiting for.

Our room was not that large to begin with, so it was a simple matter to drop to my right knee, grab under the bed, and suffer a moment of near panic when my hand did not find anything. Russ began turning in my direction when my hand closed on the stock of the rifle. It slid from between the two pillows and I brought it to bear on Russ as he finished his turn.

He exhaled loudly in a sort of repressed laugh. "Not bad, Craigie. Now what?"

I stood up, watching him closely. "Now you drop your gun, we go back and get Bree, and then she and I sail out of here," I replied in an even tone of voice. I was surprised at how calm I was. I mean, here I was, pointing a loaded gun at a pirate who had been my captor only moments ago. The surrealness of the moment gave me cause to wonder if I was dreaming or not.

He shook his head in a rueful manner. "I don't think so. I need this boat. You have my word you and your girl won't be harmed. If I don't come back, she's dead."

"You already lied to us once, and I'm not a big fan of second chances."

"You ever kill a man, kid? Or worse yet, shoot 'im, but not kill 'im? You gotta listen to his screams as he bleeds to death. Unless ya got the guts to put 'nother bullet in him. Have you?" He saw the answer on my face. "Didn't think so. And 'nother thing, you pull on me and I'll get at least a coupla shots off, so we'd both be dead. What do you think my boys would do to your lil' princess, hm? What doya think they're doin' right now to her? You have my word as a frien' of yer parents, we all walk out of this."

I did not like his tone nor the veiled threat of malice in his voice. His insinuations about Bree almost pushed me over the edge. I almost shot him then and there. In fact, I was thinking of doing just that and taking my chances. He must have realized what was going through my mind, because his eyes narrowed and he surprised me by saying, "Besides, you got a coupla small problems."

As I seemed to be holding all the cards, I gave in to his small delay of what I now assumed was his inevitable demise. "And they are?"

"You forgot to chamber a round, and your safety's on."

Surprised, I looked down, and that was when he efficiently knocked the M-4 out of my hands and slammed his weapon into the side of my head. I lay on the floor stunned, waiting for the bullet I would never hear. How quickly the tide had turned again. He was yelling something, but my ears were ringing so I could not make out the words. I deserved what I was about to get for falling for the oldest trick in the book.

The room stopped spinning and I mumbled, "You gave your word you wouldn't hurt us."

"Hello, stupid. I'm a pirate, remember? Pirates steal, cheat, kill, and above all else," he paused for dramatic effect, "Lie. Besides, all deals're off 'cause you pulled a freakin' gun on me!" I sighed and waited to die. My biggest regret was what would happen to Bree.

He surprised me by saying, "Alright, on yer feet. We're goin' back to get the rest of my crew. And your girlfriend." I did not bother correcting him.

Back into the smaller boat and back to shore. Blood trickled down the left side of my face from a cut above my ear. Back down the path and into the clearing where the other three pirates and Bree were waiting. I breathed another sigh of relief when I saw that she was safe. She threw herself into my arms and started crying. I admit I was emotional as well. "We heard three shots, and I thought … I thought …" She could not finish.

"It wasn't me. It was Caleb." I did not elaborate, nor did I need to. Bree understood.

It took three trips to get us all on board the *Madora*. Russ stayed with us, the M-4 pointed in our direction the entire time, as the other pirates were ferried back and forth. I contemplated an attempt at disarming him in the smaller boat, but he had redirected the M-4 in Bree's direction, and I did not dare to put her in jeopardy. His eyes never left me, however. Russ was a shrewd one, and he was sizing me up and judging me. I had shown him what I was capable of, and I knew he would not underestimate me again. I wondered if he would kill us on the ship and then toss our bodies overboard like he had with Caleb. I soon had my answer.

Once on board, the pirates did not raise the sails. They instead engaged the engines, and we motored at a leisurely pace to the other side of the island. We rounded a finger of land and I was surprised to see a sheltered cove that was hidden from sight of the ocean. Set further back in the trees were several small cabins in various states of disrepair, and a narrow stream emptied into the bay.

We pulled up alongside a shabby dock made of weathered gray planks and tied off. The dock did not look capable of holding Bree's weight, let alone mine. I was shocked to find that it held both of us, although there were several ominous creaks and it wobbled a bit. Bree and I exited first, and giving us about a ten foot lead, Russ followed next. I was still waiting for a bullet, despite it not making sense for him to kill us on the beach. He or one of his cronies would only have to drag our bodies somewhere else.

He snapped some orders to his men, "Jay, I want ya to go through our new ship with a fine-toothed comb. If I go in later an' find you missed somethin', you ain't gonna be happy. I want ya to scrape off the ID numbers as well, we'll get some fake ones later." He turned to the others. "Rob an' Blu, I want ya to take our guests," he said the last word as though he had tasted something foul. "For a lil' walk out in da jungle."

So this was it, the moment of truth. Bree inhaled sharply, realizing the truth and implications behind what Russ had said. I imagined our dead bodies rotting in the woods. A macabre image of a raven standing on my forehead and picking at my blistered and decaying face rose unbidden in my find. I forced it away with great effort, and it was replaced by an even worse image. I pictured Bree's corpse decomposing in the sand. There had to be a way out of this! I wracked my brain, but I was feeling sluggish and stupid.

I turned, and both Rob and the lanky pirate Russ had referred to as Blu had raised weapons pointed in our direction. They stood a dozen feet away, so there was not any chance for me to charge them and attempt to disarm or incapacitate one of them. Perhaps a better opportunity would present itself once we were in the jungle. My major concern was that Bree would try some foolish stunt and get shot in the process. I had to admit to myself that the ideas I had entertained were probably not any better than the ones she might be thinking of.

We followed a narrow, sandy path into the dense jungle. It was so narrow, in fact, that we had to walk in single file. Bree went first, then myself, followed by our two executioners Rob and Blu. I tried to slow down so that one of them would get in range for me to make a grab at their gun, but Blu gave me a violent shove forward to keep me moving. I chanced a look back over my shoulder, they had backed off as well.

"Move it, dirtball," snarled Blu. Killing us would not be any big deal for him. He might even enjoy it. He looked like the type that had drowned puppies for fun as a child.

Facing forward and throwing caution to the wind, I asked the back of Bree's head, "So, you knew both my mother and father, Rob?"

"Shut up," replied Blu. The depth and breadth of their vocabularies continued to astound me. Two word responses seemed to be their style, but I was in for another surprise.

"Aye," said Rob. I waited for Blu to say something. I guess Rob was waiting too, because when Blu remained silent, Rob continued, "Erich was the original captain when I got here. He and Cara Nichole were ... together, at that time."

Against my better judgement, I was considering asking what had happened when Blu let out a yell of pain and began cursing. Both Bree and I flinched, wasting an opportune time to make a run for it. My curiosity had gotten the better of me, and I stopped and turned around.

Blu was crouched down, his limp, greasy hair hanging in his sweat streaked face. Blood was streaming down from his right shoulder and leg, and creating a stain in the pristine sand.

"Stupid tree," he snarled. I looked back and saw the rotted, jagged, sheared off black stump which was leaning in a precarious manner over the path. Bree, Rob, and I had all ducked around it. Blu, who had been distracted or fantasizing about killing us had walked right into it. The stump had peeled back flaps of skin on his leg and shoulder as effective as any scalpel. He saw me looking at him and growled, "What're you lookin' at, pinhead?"

I wanted to explain to him that I was not the one who had walked into a tree and was in need of stitches, but my time was better spent on planning a way to get out of this. Keeping a watchful eye on us, Rob gave the bloody wound a cursory examination.

"Man, that don't look good, bro'. Mebbe we better go back to camp an' get it looked at?"

"Right," snapped Blu. "The Cap'n would really love that. Me messin' up a simple job."

"Yer bleedin' like a stuck pig, Blu."

"Thank you, Doctor Obvious. I'll just go wash off the blood. It'll scab up quick enough, and then we'll off 'em on the beach."

We veered down toward the beach and the water. I did not want to imagine what it would feel like to get salt in those wounds, but they would get disinfected in the process. On the beach and in the sand, my feet kicked up several shells. I stopped, knelt down, and picked one up. A Turnip Whelk. The ground was littered with them. This was the beach, then. This was the right island. My mother had once walked here, over twenty years ago. I shivered in the sunlight.

"Get movin'," ordered Blu. We marched down to the water's edge. Rob shouldered Blu's rifle, but kept his own pointed in our direction. Casting one last, nasty look over his shoulder, Blu said, "Ya better enjoy this break. You're not gonna be enjoyin' much of anythin', soon enough. Maybe after we do you," he gave Bree a hungry animal look. "We'll do her." I did not like what he was implying, nor was there much room for me to misinterpret it.

I made eye contact with Bree, it was desperation time. Now was our chance, one of the pirates was wading out into the ocean, and the other one was distracted and holding both guns. Bree's eyes were wide with fear, and they were a bit glassy as well. I assumed she was in a mild state of shock over what Blu had just said, coupled with everything else that had happened to us. I was on my own, then.

I looked over at Rob, who was shielding his eyes and watching Blu. I tensed the muscles in my legs, preparing to spring the several steps between us and then tackle him. I attempted to swallow, but my throat was dry, I would have only one chance. It never happened.

A piercing scream caused me to slip and tumble to the ground on my backside. It would have been comical if it had not been a matter of life or death. The scream continued, and rose several octaves before mixing with a strangling gurgling noise. I looked at the water.

The noise was emanating from Blu, who was splashing around and throwing up a spray of water. At first I thought he was screaming because of the sting from the salt water in his wounds. Then I realized he was not jumping up and down in the water, something was jerking him back and forth. My next thought he was trying to escape a jellyfish or something. Then I saw the fins. The something were sharks. There was not any mistake, they were sharks, not dolphins.

The next several minutes passed by in slow, dream-like motion. It was not anything at all like any movie I had ever seen. Blu had stopped screaming, he was pulled under twice more, he seemed to have escaped for a moment, and then was yanked under again. He surfaced in a frothy pink spray of blood and water and looked toward where the three of us were standing on the beach.

"Shoot it!" He screamed.

Rob raised his rifle to his shoulder, and I was surprised to see that it was my M-4, or one that looked like it. He did not shoot, whether it was out of concern for hitting Blu, or because it would not have made any difference at this point, I was unsure. I remembered Caleb telling me that people were normally oblivious to when they were in the water with sharks. I had even seen photographs take from a plane of swimmers completely surrounded by sharks while swimming. Ignorance was bliss, but I knew I would never swim in the ocean again. The ghost of Caleb's voice also came back from the day we had gone swimming. Most shark attacks happen in less then three feet of water. Blu had entered the water bleeding, and paid the ultimate price for his momentary lack of judgement. Then it was over.

He reached one hand toward us, and then sank slowly beneath the waves. Right before he went under, a gout of blood much larger than I would have anticipated burst from his mouth. There was a brief frenzy of fins in the water, and then a wave broke over the spot and Blu was gone. It had taken all of maybe five minutes by my reckoning.

When it was over, Rob stared at Bree and me for a long moment. He seemed to be thinking, a pensive look on his face. Was he going to kill us now, and feed our bloody bodies to the sharks? I again tensed to make a leap at him, but his words shocked me to immobility.

"We're going back to camp. We'll take the scenic route. I want to tell you a story." Again he paused. "I'll lead, but don't think of tryin' anything stupid." We entered the jungle in silence.

CHAPTER 9

▼

We walked in silence for a ways, although the jungle was never truly silent for long. There was an almost steady hum of insects, screeching faint bird calls echoed through the trees, gusts of wind would set the palms whispering, and we could still hear the ocean. The sun shone through the trees making a lacy pattern on our bodies and the ground as we walked. I was still unsure whether or not Rob was still planning on killing us, but somehow I doubted that he would. He had several opportunities to do so, and had not taken any of them. I also did not believe that he was simply going to let us go free, but I clung to that faint hope like a drowning man clings to a life preserver in rough seas.

He took a deep breath and began, "Your mother—Cara Nichole, had been here a couple of months before Jake—Jay, as he's now called, and I showed up on the scene. He and I had been hangin' out at a local bar on another island a couple hours from here, an' in walked Erich. He approached us, and asked us if we were lookin' for work, and hired the two of us on the spot." Rob sighed at the memory of that day, twenty years ago. "He told us that there would be some danger and risk involved, but Jay and I were not exactly law-abiding citizens to begin with, if you know what I mean."

Here, he paused. I think he was trying to collect his thoughts. Neither Bree nor I spoke, not wanting to interrupt him. "He also hired Russ that day. Jay and I knew of him, but we weren't exactly what you would call pals or anything. Russ was trouble. He drank almost twenty-four/seven, and got into fights easily. He—he cut up one guy real bad one night out-side the bar. But Erich seemed to think he was okay, I guess. Maybe he thought he could keep him under control, I don't know. We'd also seen Erich around a couple of times, too."

Rob pushed back a palm frond and it snapped back, hitting me in the face. I wiped at my watery eyes, trying to soothe the stinging. When my vision cleared, I realized that I was now right behind him, and that he had slung the M-4 over his shoulder. I stared at the back of his wrinkled, sun-burned neck. It would be an almost simple matter to hit him from behind and disarm him while he was engrossed in telling this story. However, he was demonstrating trust in us by leading, and more importantly, he was telling us the potential truth about what had happened to my parents all those years ago.

"Erich brought us back here, and that's when I met your mother for the first time." I looked around us, and the jungle pressed in close and thick on all sides. Sliding back and vanishing into the forest was not an option at this time, and we would have been lost anyway. "Your mother was some-thing else," he glanced back at me. "No offense."

"None taken. Thanks for telling us all of this. I never knew the whole story."

"Oh, there's more, believe me." He chuckled and then drew another deep breath. "Erich had Cara Nichole pick our brains to see if we were on the up and up, so to speak. It's been over twenty years, but I can still see her on the beach that day." He closed his eyes for a moment, in memory. It was obvious that my mother had made an indelible impression on him, and I was left wondering how I could use that information to help Bree and me to escape.

"So, a coupla days later, Russ comes up missin'. Cara Nichole was busy tending Erich's shoulder from when he had been shot a couple of weeks before. It was infected I think, his shoulder, I mean. He'd been shot dur-ing a raid on another ship that went bad. He had also lost a coupla crew members that day, as well. That's why he brought us on board."

A crash came from our left and the three of us jumped, and then froze in silence, listening. Rob raised an eyebrow and looked back at us again, "If a tree falls in the forest ... Anyway, we had one of our famous storms before we could find Russ." He paused again in his story. "I'm not really sure of the facts here. According to Russ, who was hiding in the woods and about to raid our camp, he caught your parents running through the jungle. Whether they were planning on leaving together, or if Erich was just trying to get your mom off the island, I don't know. Did you ever notice Russ is missing his front teeth?"

I nodded. I had noticed much about Russ, and most of it had not been good. I also wondered much about him. Why would others follow his lead? And what type of men would take orders from someone like that? The more answers I discovered, the more questions I had.

"Well, according to Russ, and he was drunk at the time when he shared this with me, your mother kicked out one of his teeth, and your father knocked out the other." Rob gave a genuine laugh. "It definitely sounds like something they would do, and he's only ever told that story once, at least when I was around." The smile faded from his face as quickly as it had arrived.

"Russ was with another group of pirates. Erich once told me there were several hundred in this area alone. He also said that sometimes they would raid each other, it was safer than risking tangling with the authorities. The group Russ was in wanted what we had. They attacked just as the storm was ending. They would have taken us completely by surprise if your mother hadn't screamed out a warning. We never found her body, so we just took it for granted that she was among the dead that we couldn't find."

I asked my first question. "Why did she stay with him as long as she did?"

"No mistake, kid. Your parents loved each other. It was as plain as day whenever they were around each other or looked at each other. Erich was either leaving with her, or making her leave because he suspected somethin' was up with Russ. He didn't want her in any more danger than she needed to be in. Maybe if they had known she was pregnant with you ..."

"I don't think she found that out until she was back in the states," I supplied.

Rob nodded. "Makes sense, I guess. She never woulda left—alone anyway, if she had known they were in a family way. They were very loyal to each other. The whole 'if you love something, set it free' and all that."

I shivered, remembering when my mother had said almost those exact same words to me.

"What happened to my father, Rob?"

He gave me a cautious look. "I think you already know the answer to that."

"Still, I want to hear it. Call it closure, if you will."

Rob lowered his head and continued walking. "He and Russ had a fight. I think that if Erich had been a hundred percent he would've mopped the floor with Russ. But that injured shoulder really slowed him down. In the end, Russ was just toying with him, and without Cara Nichole around, Erich didn't even seem to care. Russ killed him in front of all of us."

He was silent a long moment. "Those of us who were left, Jay, myself, a coupla others, were given a choice. We could join up with Russ and his crew, or we could end up like Erich. We had wiped out a lot of his guys in that battle, so he was hurting for a crew. We also sank their ship, and they sank Erich's. A coupla weeks later we were able to cobble together a sloop that we used for raiding, but it wasn't very effective. We weren't very successful or lucky either. Over the years, Russ couldn't find anyone to replace lost crew. The authorities had also stepped up surveillance in the area, and a lot of vacationers are now traveling armed." He shrugged. "Our last ship sank a coupla months ago, an' we've been stuck on land ever since."

"How did you survive?" asked Bree. I was wondering that myself.

Rob gave a rueful laugh. "They usta have a thing called the South Beach Diet. Well, we went on the Bermuda Triangle Diet. There's a lot of things around here that you can eat—if you can keep 'em down, that is. We were more worried about Scurvy than starving, though."

Anticipating the question I was about to ask, he continued, "Scurvy is a Vitamin C deficiency. In the old days it usta wipe out entire crews of ships that who on long trips. It's not such a big deal now-a-days, but there's not a whole lotta oranges around. In fact there's none."

"How did you manage to catch us?" I was unable to keep the disbelief from my voice.

"We're not as dumb or as helpless as you think. We're always watching the water with binoculars for signs of a ship or the Coast Guard patrols. Blu saw you guys anchor off shore and then motor on over. It was a simple ambush for us to set up after that. You made a lotta noise walkin' in the woods. Russ was gettin' pretty desperate for a ship at that point, and the rest of us were getting pretty sick of Russ. In the old days of pirating, the ships were a democracy, and captains were voted in and out all the time."

"I'm guessing that wasn't an option with Russ?"

Rob shook his head in the negative. "I've only seen two people stand up to him, and they're both dead, and he obviously is not. I keep my mouth shut and follow orders."

Unsure if I wanted an answer or not, I asked, "Like the order you were given about us?"

"That's different. Losing Blu like that, well, that changes things. Russ may be lookin' for a new crew member or two."

"Me? A pirate?" I almost laughed at the absurdity of that. "Bree and I have a life all planned out that we want to go back to." Remembering her nausea, I added, "As well as other reasons we want and need to go home."

"Bein' a pirate is in your blood, Justin. As for Bree," he looked back at the two of us. "Did anyone ever tell you that she bears a striking resemblance to your mother?"

We shook our heads in unison. Bree did not remind me of my mother at all in the physical sense. True, both were strong women with a sense of humor and a love for others, but I did not think that they looked alike. Maybe Rob's memory was playing tricks on him, or he had been on this island for far too long.

"Well, Bree is a bit curvier, if you will, but there are some similarities."

I did not respond to that. I did not think that he was being a pig about it, he was just stating the facts as he saw them. It struck me that he was not like Russ, and therefore, we might be able to appeal to him.

"Look, Rob. Why don't you just let us go? You know that Russ wants us dead, he even told me so. You're not like him. Do it for my mother and father."

He appeared to contemplate this proposal for a long moment before answering, "But I am like Russ. I've done things I'm not proud of, sure, but …" He slowed down, realizing the precarious situation he might be in by having us walk behind him. "Mebbe you guys should walk in front of me for a bit. The trail's pretty easy through here."

We stepped back and switched places. He had removed the rifle from off his shoulder, and now held it in an easy, confident manner cradled in one arm. It was another opportunity lost, and I cursed myself silently for not taking him out when I'd had the chance earlier. I had an idea that chances to escape were running out fast.

"If you're like Russ, then why didn't you kill us earlier?"

"I told you, we might be able to strike a deal where you join us. Russ needs new crew members. We need youth and energy. We're all old men …" This last was said with regret, almost as if by admitting it, it was becoming true to him. "Bree may be a problem, though. Women and ships are considered unlucky by most sailors."

"No Bree, no me." I was not truly entertaining the idea of joining them, but I wanted to humor him if would help us escape. I tried to make my voice sound tough, "That's an M-4 you're carrying, I've been trained to use one. I'm going to count to three, and then I'm going to take it from you, or you're going to have to shoot me right now."

"No, Justin," cautioned Bree. I could hear in her voice that she thought I might try it.

"No, Justin," repeated Rob, as I stopped, turned and faced him. "If I have to, I'll shoot you in the leg, and we can drag you outta here."

"Shooting me in the leg won't stop me."

"No, but it will slow you down. An' if you're injured, or dead, who's gonna protect Bree from Russ and the others?"

Others? I had not seen any others. It had just been the four of them. "What others?"

"There's two other pirates here. Their names are Nicky and Carlos. They're out in the jungle standing guard and watching the ocean." He abruptly changed the subject. "Your father had one of these." He patted the M-4 like an obedient dog. "Great weapon, it's good in close combat, too. As well as conditions like these. Although the salt water can make 'em jam if you don't keep them clean."

So there were six pirates. Rob, Jay, Russ, Nicky, Carlos, and … There had been six pirates I amended. Now there were five. The information about the sentries was also pertinent. If Bree and I did manage to escape, we would have to be on the watch for them as well. This was getting more difficult by the moment. I realized that Bree and Rob were right about it being foolish for me to attempt to disarm him. He would shoot me, and then this would become even more complicated. I held up my hands, palms out, and turned back around and resumed walking.

"Tell me about my father, Rob?"

"Erich?" I sensed his shrug behind me. "What do you want to know about him?" When I did not answer, he simply plowed on. "You look just like him. When we surprised you in the jungle you had your backs to us at first. When you turned around, I thought for a moment …" He gave a nervous laugh, "I thought I was seein' his ghost. I'll bet I'm not the only one, either. You're lucky Russ didn't shoot ya on the spot."

"He said he needed me to get our boat. He killed our …" What had Caleb been? I thought of what a pain in the neck he had been, but he also had saved our lives as well. People like Caleb can no more change the way they are then a tiger can change its stripes. I admitted out loud and to myself the truth. "Russ killed our friend."

"Aye. He needed you for bait, although if Russ could've kept her quiet, Bree would've worked just as well. As for your friend …" He was silent for a long moment. Then realizing that there was not anything he could say that would change the facts of the matter, he shrugged it off. I felt a moment of sorrow for Caleb. He had been a unique individual. I wondered what he had been like when he was younger. Had he been obnoxious and disgusting? Had his sense of humor changed over time? I pictured him as a class clown in school, making others laugh, usually at someone else's expense, and always keeping the teachers on their toes. He had mentioned a wife and kids as well. Rob interrupted my musings on Caleb.

"Erich Craigie was a good man. He was loyal to his friends, honest, and he treated us all fairly and as equals. I don't know," he shrugged. "I only knew him for a short time, but he sure seemed to love your mom." He laughed. "There I go repeatin' myself, but it's true. Whenever they were together they couldn't keep their eyes off each other. They were like two teenagers in love."

I tried a different tactic. "What about the M-4? If you give it back to me the three of us can escape."

Yeah, right. I give you a gun and we just stroll into camp and let Russ pick us off. Pow, pow, pow."

I swallowed the lump in my throat at those three one syllable words, and then tried again.

"If we got rid of Russ, then you could be in charge. You could be the captain."

"Captain of what? We still wouldn't have a ship." There was not much conviction in his voice, and I thought frantically. It was a chance, however slim though it might be.

"Russ mentioned dropping me and Bree off near a shipping lane and keeping the *Madora*. He was probably lying, but we could strike a similar deal between us."

"Ya, sure. Then you go to the Coast Guard, come back, get your ship, and me and my crew all go to jail for a long time. Thanks, but no thanks. I'm forty something years old, and spending the rest of my life behind bars just doesn't sound like a very good plan to me."

I realized that there was not anything I could say or do that would change his mind. I looked at Bree and raised an eyebrow, maybe she could rationalize and convince him.

"Rob," she began in a slow, even tone of voice. "You said that Justin and I remind you of his mother and father. It's obvious that you held both of them in high regard and cared a great deal for them. Do you want to see what happened to them happen to us as well? You're a good man, Rob. Despite what you may have done in your past. I can tell that …"

"I. Don't. Want. To. Hear. This." He bit off each word through clenched teeth.

Bree stopped and crossed her arms. I knew that look well. "Rob, I'm …" And then she said it out loud, "Pregnant." I exhaled loudly. I had suspected it, but now here it was. Bree was not bluffing or trying to trick him. We both heard the honesty in her voice. I was momentarily overwhelmed by a myriad of emotions. I was going to be a father! I heard her finish up,

"What kind of place is this to raise a baby? Let alone have one?"

We walked several dozen steps in silence. I tried to put myself in Rob's shoes. What was he thinking? What would he do? It was not truly a fair analogy, however, my morals and values were much different than his. Or were they?

"I'd like to help you," there was resignation in his voice. "Really. But I can't. I'm sorry."

I chewed on my lip in pensive, reflective thought. Had we attempted all avenues at our disposal? I could not think of any other rationalizations or justifications. Begging and pleading did not seem to work either. The overwhelming thought that Bree was carrying our child kept pushing all other thoughts away from my mind. Would it be a boy or a girl? It did not matter. What would the baby look like? A mix of both of us? I hoped it would have her eyes and hair. In my mind I pictured a tan, fair-haired child playing in the gentle waves as they broke along the beach. Would our son or daughter be an athlete? Would he or she do well in school? What would they grow up to be? A doctor? A lawyer? A marine biologist like my mother? My mind skipped from one question to the next, and I was so proud that there were tears in my eyes.

I reached over and took Bree's hand and squeezed. She turned and I mouthed those three little but important words to her that I made sure I told her several times a day so that she would not forget how I felt. She smiled and winked at me, and there were tears in her eyes as well. Names began running through my head, both boy names and girl names. Then I forced those pleasant thoughts away with great effort and reluctance. We needed to get out of this mess first. That was what I needed to focus on, not our unborn miracle.

Rob broke in with what I thought at first was a random statement. "When we get back to camp, one of the first cabins you'll see used to be your mother's when she was here. Although it's a lot more run down now then it used to be. The whole camp is falling apart. It's not easy to keep things up and runnin' when you're not gettin' any supplies to take care of things. Yet another example of the difference in how Russ runs things and how Erich used to do it."

"It sounds like you're not a big fan of the way Russ is running things around here."

He looked around warily for a moment to see who might be listening before he answered, "Like I said before, he's not real strong in the leadership department. He's killed more crew members 'cause of his temper than we ever lost in all the raids, combined. None of those who are left really care for him, but also nobody dares to stand up to him, alone or as a group."

"Why not?" I realized I was being overly inquisitive, to the point of being nosey, but it just did not make any sense to me at all. "Why don't you just get rid of him?"

"Your mother used to ask a lot of difficult questions without easy answers, too. You don't understand. Things are ... things are different out here—on this island. The rules of society just don't apply to us. Better a leader who rules through fear, than no leader at all."

A flash of bright color among the green and brown trees distracted me. It was some type of bird. I was surprised at the amount of diverse life out here. I wondered where it all came from, and how it survived? The weather alone would kill most animals, I thought. Another tangent which only served to waste what precious little time we had left. I was angry with myself for wasting my energy and time on ornithological pursuits. I should be thinking of a way to escape rather than looking at birds. The anger was also unproductive, I realized.

I could turn and charge Rob. I might catch him off guard and be able to get the rifle before he shot me. Would he shoot me? He had implied that he was not a law abiding citizen and would go to jail if he was captured by the authorities. Could Bree or I distract him? It would have to be Bree in order for me to have a chance to disarm him. What if he yelled for help? I would have to knock him out or kill him as fast as possible. Both were risky, it would have to be fast. If I missed, he could alert someone else or injure one of us. How would I communicate this plan to Bree?

Another option was to simply wait until we got back to camp. Rob had suggested we might be able to reason with Russ. He might agree to letting us live if we stayed. Not that I would stay, but if we could convince them that we were, maybe we could gain their trust and make our escape later. This plan was a bit more risky. Was it even possible to reason with Russ? I suspected that he was slightly off balance to begin with. I was not even certain how he would react once he realized Rob had disobeyed an order and that we were still alive. I had an idea that he would not take it very well. Would Rob be able to reason with him? So far, I was creating more questions than answers and solutions.

We could also wait until we got back to the pirate camp and then attempt to take the initiative. I contemplated trying to take the M-4 from Rob and then disposing of Russ myself. It was apparent that this was not a very good option either. It put both Bree and I in great danger, and I was also unsure as to whether or not I would actually be able to shoot someone else. Seeing as how I was not that accurate a shot to begin with myself, what if I missed? What if I succeeded in disarming Rob or one of the others, and the rifle jammed? Or if I forgot to thumb off the safety again? I exhaled loudly in frustration, and ran my fingers through my sweaty hair. Bree gave my hand another reassuring squeeze. I had to protect her, and our child.

Was I missing out on any courses of action? There was always the old 'hope for the best' strategy. I did not think that this was a viable option. After all, I had seen Russ shoot down Caleb in cold blood. Rob had also alluded to their violent lifestyle. These were men who lived by their own set of laws, who lived and existed outside of social expectations and norms.

I needed a plan, and I needed one soon if we were going to get out of this. We must almost be back at camp by now. Panic was becoming a tight, hard knot in my stomach. Or maybe it was fear.

I contemplated wrestling with Rob for control of the rifle again. I chanced a glance back at him. We made eye contact and he nodded his head at me. I visualized grabbing the M-4 and the tussle that would ensue. I would yell for Bree to run, and once she was safely away I would take the rifle from Rob. He was twice my age and half starved, how strong could he be? Once I had regained possession of the weapon, I would have to silence him. I knew that I would not be able to shoot him, that would alert the others. I would have to subdue and silence him quickly and quietly, before he could yell out a warning. Hitting him the head with the stock of the gun was an idea.

Bree and I would reunite in the jungle. If they pursued us we would find higher ground with several escape routes possible. No, wait, that was not a good idea. Armies would historically surround and then flank their enemies. But if we had our backs against a cliff we would be trapped. We needed to find a place we could defend if we needed to, that would also allow us to retreat if it came to that. Of course, the pirates knew the layout of the island better than we did. I did have twenty rounds in the clip of my M-4, that was four shots for each pirate.

If they did not pursue us, we would need a ship. The *Madora* was the only one to be had. They knew that as well. We would have to surprise them and hope for the best, we did not have any other choice. Caleb had showed us both how to run the engines, sailing was not an option.

We ended up not having a choice. I had slowed down, and was beginning to turn so that I could charge Rob. I had taken a breath so that I could yell for Bree to run as well. From just ahead of us came a loud metal clashing, and male voices shouting curses.

"Here goes nothing," said Rob.

We had returned to the pirate camp.

CHAPTER 10

▼

The sandy path beneath our feet passed between a few more sparse and stunted palm trees, and then we were in the camp itself. At first my eyes refused to believe what they were seeing. Russ and Jake were sparring with swords, or cutlasses, or whatever they were called. That was what had caused the metal ringing sound we had heard moments ago. As they fought, the sound of the two blades striking each other had reverberated throughout the woods.

There was food and drink set out along a rough wooden table on one side of the clearing. The pirates were either in the process of eating lunch, or were just finishing up. I noticed a pistol and several rifles on the table as well, and my eyes narrowed in thought. My options had increased. I also counted all five pirates in the clearing. My odds decreased. What had happened to two of them standing watch at all times? I assumed now that they had a new ship they were not being as cautious.

I glanced down at the harbor where the *Madora* was moored. She bobbed in the gentle waves like a toy. Escape and salvation were that close. I took another good look around the camp. There were three small cabins in various states of disrepair. Off to one side there was a larger building as well. Two other very rough buildings lay like afterthoughts at the edge of the jungle. A fast moving, narrow stream ran along one border of the camp.

I looked up in time to see Russ bat away Jake's weapon with a ringing clash. Then he noticed us and lowered his own sword. Silence descended among the men as everyone ceased talking and turned our way. Russ turned from a blotchy red from his exertions to an almost purple color as he launched into an apoplectic tirade fueled by rage.

"I ain't believin' this! What are they doin' still alive? I gave you an order! And when I give an order, I expect it to be followed without any freakin' questions!" He dropped his sword into the sand and snatched up a pistol off one of the tables. Clenching his fists and facial muscles in anger, he marched over to where we stood, and pointed the pistol at Rob's head.

"Gimme one reason, just one, why I shouldn't kill you right now for disobeyin' a direct order from your captain? You know," he emphasized the second word. "What the penalty is for not doing what I tell you." It was not a question. I did not need to be told what the penalty was. If this is how he ran things, I was surprised that there were any of his crew left at all.

To Rob's credit he remained calm. He did lick his lips once, and I did notice a line of sweat bead and run down from his forehead. His voice however, remained cool when he answered, "If you kill me, you'll be down two crew members instead of just one."

"What!" Screeched Russ, spraying Rob's face with spittle. He was fast approaching an entire new level of rage. At this rate, we would not have to worry about getting rid of him, he would cause himself to have a stroke or heart attack if he continued on like this, if he did not kill us all first.

"Blu got hit by a shark. He caught himself on a snag in the woods and was washing off the blood in the ocean when it happened. I thought that maybe ..."

"You thought? You don't think around here, you do what you're told. And I told you to get rid of them!" He gestured toward us with the hand holding the pistol. Bree and I both flinched at the violence and malice that filled his voice.

"Maybe they would be willing to join us," pleaded Rob. "God knows we need more people, we need new people. We need some youth."

"Ya, right," snorted Russ. "And how long do you think they," he sneered the word, "would stay here before trying to escape? Or kill us as revenge for his," he nodded in my direction, "father? Look at 'em! They're soft! They're weak! They wouldn't last ten minutes out here, let alone on a raid!"

He turned and the pistol was now pointed at me. The bore seemed huge, and it was like looking down a very dark tunnel. I realized with a sick fascination that if he was not holding my actual Glock pistol, it was one that looked very similar to it. How ironic that I was about to be killed with a weapon I had bought to protect us. Despite all of my elaborate plans, this was how it was going to end. I did not have time nor room to do anything.

"How 'bout it, pretty boy? You wanna be a big, bad pirate like your dad?"

"No." He laughed at my monosyllabic answer. "We just want to be let go. We want to go home." Even I could hear the near whine in my voice. I think that this pleased him, my meaningless pleading that would not change a thing. "If you let us go we promise to never say anything about what we've seen or heard."

"Oh, really?" He seemed to be considering my proposal. "How stupid do you think I am?" I did not have time to answer the rhetorical question. I doubt that he would have appreciated my answer anyway. "I have a better idea," he started, his eyes gleaming. Knowing that I was not going to like his idea, I waited in silence for him to continue.

"You see our sword collection?" Not taking his eyes off me, jerked one thumb over his shoulder. I nodded. "We practice with those, because these," he turned the pistol in his grip, examining it. "Ain't always reliable."

Without warning or preamble he jerked his arm up, pointed the pistol at me, and pulled the trigger. There was a loud click, which was drowned out by a scream from Bree. I closed my eyes and tried to draw a normal breath, but that simple action was proving to be very difficult. There was not any tremendous explosion like I had imagined, although there was a loud ringing in my ears. It took a tremendous effort for me to open my eyes. I looked down and was surprised not to see any bloody holes in my body. Russ stepped back with an evil grin.

"Fer instance, that one wasn't even loaded." Seeing the murderous intent in my eyes, he ticked a finger back and forth in warning. "Mm-mm. You ain't heard my idea yet. Oh, yer gonna love it, if you are your father's son." Still keeping an eye on me, he knelt down and picked up the sword he had dropped earlier. He turned and plucked another one off the table.

"You an' I are gonna have a little old fashioned sword fight. If you win, you and your girl get to go home. When I win," he held my gaze for a long moment. "And I will win, my problems 'bout what to do with you will be solved."

In a shaky voice I asked, "Is it to the … to the death?"

Russ laughed. "No, we'll just go until one of us yells 'uncle.' Of course it's to the death, stupid. We're pirates, remember?" So saying, he tossed the other rusty blade at my feet.

"And if I refuse to fight you?" I already knew the answer, but I was stalling for time. It was apparent that I was going to need a new plan in a hurry.

"Then you're dead. And so is she." He gestured toward Bree.

Keeping a watchful eye on him, I knelt and picked up the sword. There was some sand on the handle, and the blade did not look all that keen. I could not count on him to fight in a fair manner. He would fight dirty, and use every nasty trick he knew. I would need to be prepared for anything. I started to stand and that was when he launched his first attack on me.

Just in time I lifted the clumsy cumbersome blade and was lucky enough to block his initial swing. He had brought the sword over his head and using two hands, brought it crashing down onto my blade, almost as if he was swinging an ax. There was a ringing crash which brought cheers from the other pirates who were watching with rapt attention. The vibration numbed my arm in an instant. As he spun to recover, still on my hands and knees, I scrambled back like a retreating crab and put some distance between us.

I rose to my feet and hefted the sword. It was heavier than I had expected it to be, and I needed both hands to hold it up. Russ moved hypnotically to my left, I side-stepped, trying to keep him in front of me. The point of his blade moved in intricate patterns in the air. I caught myself watching the sword tip instead of him. I removed a sweaty hand from the sandy handle of the sword and wiped it on my shorts. It would not be good if I dropped the sword because my hands were slick with perspiration or sand. Successful, I tried to switch to my other hand.

Russ attacked again. I did not have time to react. There was a searing, burning pain across my left bicep. I darted a quick look down, a line of blood had appeared as if by magic.

"Ah, first blood." Russ bragged smugly. "Are you afraid yet? You know you can't win."

Again we circled each other. The blood beaded and began to run down my arm. He was right. I did not stand a chance against him. I did not have any experience in hand to hand combat. It was not my own well being that I was concerned about, however.

"If you do beat me, let my fiancee go."

"Not a chance." He faked a lunge and I backed up, almost tripping over a pile of sand.

"If I win," I panted. "How do I know your crew still won't kill us?" How had I gotten out of breath so fast? Before this, I had figured myself to be in good shape. I figured wrong.

He gave the other pirates a sideways glance. "They go free if he wins, but we keep the sailboat."

His attention elsewhere, I leapt forward and stabbed in his direction. He easily parried my blow, and got one of his own in. Again the pain, only this time across my right shoulder.

"Such a good try." Good, but futile. And he had scored on me again in the process. "This is how your father died, Justin. Just like this." He emphasized the last three words. A lazy flick of his wrist opened a cut across my forearm. He was toying with me, like a cat with a mouse. The sword seemed heavier, and I was now gasping for air.

"Have you heard of a death by a thousand cuts?" He asked in a conversational tone. "Each cut is small, meaningless, but when you add 'em all up ..." Another flick, but I saw it coming and was barely able to block it. It was a combination attack however, and he dipped his sword tip, grazing the right quadricep on my leg.

"I killed your father like this," he repeated. "He didn't last to a thousand cuts, but it was very close." His voice had lowered to a murmur, and seemed to be coming from a distance. "He fought me to the end, tho' he was mostly bled out when he finally collapsed in the sand. I looked into his helpless eyes, just like I'm lookin' in yours right now, and then I killed him." He made a big production out of examining his sword. "With this very sword, wasn't it Carlos?" The other pirate did not bother to answer. The clearing was very quiet, it was only a matter of time.

"Are you gettin' tired, Justin? You slowin' down? Do you feel yer life runnin' out of your body?" I did. All of the above. I did not answer him, instead choosing to save what little energy and breath I had left. I lowered my sword tip until it touched the sand, and wiped at my sweaty face. The back of my hand came away smeared with blood. When had he cut me up high? The afternoon was getting blurry, and the camp spun a slow circle. I was dizzy, and close to passing out. If I did, it would then be a simple matter for him to dispatch of me.

Bree had remained quiet the entire time. Out of the corner of my eye, I saw that she had edged toward the table that held the other guns. I contemplated shaking my head to discourage her, but that would give her away and put her life in jeopardy. The other pirates had formed a loose semi-circle around us, wanting to watch the grande finale. It was almost over. Maybe my death would serve as enough distraction to allow her to get to one of the guns and then shoot Russ.

And maybe not. My mouth was as dry as the sand we were fighting on. I noticed with mounting horror that there were scattered dark spots here and there on the ground. My blood. I did not have much hope of holding out much longer, but if my death contributed to Bree's freedom, then I would not have died in vain, for nothing. It would be worth it. I was nonchalant for some strange reason about the prospect of my own mortality. I did not have one of those entire life flashing in front of my eyes experiences either. Instead, I remembered the day that I had proposed to Bree. A smile cracked my face. Que sera, sera,

"What're you grinnin' about?" Snarled Russ. "Don't matter, you'll be dead, soon."

If that was the case, then so be it. I wanted to give Bree the time she needed to get to one of the weapons and then use it. I had to distract all of the pirates in order for her to do so. This is for you, Bree, I thought. Summoning up the last of my strength, I let out with a primeval roar that surprised even me, and charged Russ. I used the same overhead two-handed attack he had first used on me.

If he had been prepared, it would have been a simple matter for him to just run me through. As it was, I surprised him. My forward momentum did not allow me time to bring my sword down to strike him. Instead, I crashed into him, and we both fell to the ground in a spray of sand. I was vaguely aware of his sword spinning off to one side, about ten feet away. I rolled to my feet, gasping for air, bright spots flashing in front of my eyes. By some miracle I was still holding onto my sword. I had done it! Russ had a bloody welt along one cheek, and down across his chest. He sat in the sand looking dazed and confused.

I took a deep, shaky breath, and raised my sword. The tip was now pointed at my adversary's head. "It's over, Russ. You lose."

He laughed and nodded his head, and I felt relief wash over me like a refreshing wave of water. Then he stopped laughing and looked up to where I was standing, not ten feet away.

"No, it's not over." He pulled a pistol out from the back of his pants and pointed it at me. I had time to think that this one was probably loaded. I have heard that you do not hear the sound of the shot that kills you, but I heard it very clearly. Everything slowed down, and there was a flash and a thunderous roar. I was thrown back another dozen feet and crashed into the sand. My reflexes had locked my grip, so I lay on the ground, partially turned to one side, still holding onto my sword. I was surprised to find that I could see some sky. It was so blue.

"Now, it's over."

As I had landed facing into the camp, I was able to hear Bree scream, and then watched in horror as she lunged in the direction of Russ. Her arm described a wide arc and flashed down so that it looked almost as if she was punching him in the shoulder. He grunted, and then screamed in pain. His right arm swung out and he backhanded her away from him. A kitchen knife had sprouted as if by magic from his left shoulder. It took a minute, but I realized that she had stabbed him. There had not been time for her to grab a firearm. Seeing me get shot, and assuming I was dead, she had grabbed the nearest weapon and struck. He raised the pistol in Bree's direction, to where she lay sprawled on the ground. I tried to yell out a warning to no avail. From point blank range he fired three times into my fiancee's body. Her body trembled each time, and then lay motionless. The love of my life was dead.

Someone else was screaming, as if from a great distance. I realized that it was my voice that I was hearing, a scream of indescribable loss and anger was issuing wordlessly from my mouth. This could not be happening! It had to be some sort of horrific nightmare, and I struggled toward a consciousness that would not arrive. This was my reality, and it was all my doing, all my fault. My scream faded away, sounding like a strangled animal.

"You," sneered Russ, looking in my direction. He yanked the bloody butter knife out of his shoulder and tossed it with disdain to the ground. He stumbled over to his sword, and retrieved it from the ground. Without a word he raised it above his head for the final coup de grace. He charged across the clearing screaming his own battle cry to finish me off.

I was waiting for him. He did not realize that I still had my sword. Right before he reached me, I dragged myself to a kneeling position, and raised the tip of my sword up to meet his charge. He realized too late that I had not made the same mistake as he had made earlier. He tried to slow down or turn, but his indecision cost him dearly. His forward momentum caused him to impale himself on my sword the length of the blade, and all the way up to the very handle. He dropped his own sword, and stood there staring at me with an open mouth.

Using the handle of my sword for leverage, I pulled myself up to a standing position. We made eye contact for a long moment, both of us breathing hard, and then he blinked and slurred,

"You are your father's son." There was pain in his voice, and it pleased me.

"You're damn right I am." I twisted hard in a clockwise direction on the handle of my sword. He opened his eyes wide for a moment, and then, using both hands, I yanked back and forth on the grip, opening him up. Warm blood and entrails washed across my hands and forearms. I released the handle, and he collapsed to the ground. Unlike a lot of bad movies that I had seen when I was younger, he did not get back up. Nor would he ever rise again.

I fell to the ground as well. I may have passed out for a moment, I had lost a lot of blood. Then I was crawling across the sand to where Bree lay. She was terribly still, but when I made it to her side, she was still alive.

Her eyes were open, and reminding me of my mother that fateful day in the hospital, she weakly raised her hand and caressed my face.

"You got here … just … just in time." She whispered in a weak voice, and I knew the awful truth. Tears began flowing down my face, mixing with blood as well. I tried to finish our inside joke, and coughed back at the pain I was feeling.

"I've heard it a thousand times, Bree."

She smiled. "Nine hundred from me." And then she did die. She seemed to sink into the sand a bit, and her eyes grew empty. Our unborn child died with her, and a part of me died as well. I wanted to die, there was not anything left for me. I collapsed beside her.

An indeterminate amount of time later, I awoke in a strange bed, in a strange room. Rob and Jay were sitting by the bed, watching me. I struggled to sit up, ready to fight them off if I needed to, knowing I would not last very long against two of them, and not caring if I did.

"Hey, hey, easy …" said Rob, as if he were reassuring an injured animal. "You're gonna to be okay, kid."

I sincerely doubted that. The pain I was in confirmed that this was certainly not a dream. Then it all came rushing back. The battle, and Bree.

"How long," I rasped. "How long have I been out of it?"

"A coupla hours," replied Jay. "We bandaged you up as best we could." Indeed they had, but why? "You'll live," an uncomfortable pause. "Are you up for a walk? We have some unpleasant business to take care of."

After everything that had happened, they were still going to kill me. It did not matter, I no longer cared anymore. I just wanted it to be over, this had been more than anyone could be expected to bear. I nodded and they helped me up to a standing position and half walked, half carried me to the door. It was early evening, and the rest of the pirates were sitting in the clearing waiting for us. Two of them were holding a bloody, blanket wrapped body.

We began a silent march into the forest, and I noticed that my bandages had soaked through in spots as well, and were beginning to draw the attention of fat, black flies.

"We have to bury her in higher ground, otherwise the grave fills up with water." I looked at Rob, and he answered my unasked question, "We dragged Russ out into the jungle and left him. Let the animals have him, he doesn't deserve a proper burial."

We came to a small clearing on top of a hill. There were a dozen scattered graves in a small cemetery. Rob nodded in the direction of one that stood in the center.

"That's your father's grave."

I did not cry for Erich because I knew that he and my mother were together again at last. Just as I knew that Bree and I would be together again some day. It had taken me all this time to finally make my peace with God, but what a price I had paid, what a price.

They began to dig a hole, and in the soft dirt it did not take long. They switched off as well, when two of them grew tired, the other two would take their places. When the pirates judged that the hole was deep enough, they lowered Bree's body into it and looked up at me expectantly.

With dry eyes—I did not have any more tears to shed, nor would I ever again, I whispered, "I loved Bree Hawthorne with every fiber in my being. I will never love like that again. Goodbye, Bree." I turned away, not wanting to watch them cover her with earth. But I was still able to hear the soft sounds as the dirt struck her body.

Rob and Jake each stood on one side of me, and again helped carry me back toward camp. Carlos and Nicky were ahead of us, and because the three of us were moving quite slowly, they soon put some distance between us.

Rob cleared his throat, and seemed to be struggling with finding the words to say what was on his mind. At last, he blurted, "You're the captain now, Justin."

I heard the shock in my own voice, "Me? Captain?"

"Aye. The four of us talked it over while you were out. We voted, like we were supposed to, and it was unanimous. You have your father's charisma, people will follow you. It's your legacy. It's what you were born to do." He cut off my protest by raising his hand. "Just think about it a bit before you answer. If you want, we'll return you to civilization, but what's really left for you to go back to?" He repeated, "Think about it."

He was right of course. I had lost my mother, father, and ... Bree. There was not really anything or anyone that I truly cared about to make me want to return back to civilization. So I did think about it, and I decided to stay.

978-0-595-47810-1
0-595-47810-7